Track 9

Track 9

Sue Rovens

ISBN: 1544012292
ISBN 13: 9781544012292

Acknowledgements

A *Very Special Thank You* to all of the people on this page who contributed through the Kickstarter Campaign and helped usher this book into the world. I couldn't have done this without their help.

Carol and Dr. Stephen Cann

James Semmelroth Darnell

Charlie "The Quaker" Edwards

Mary Lynn Edwards

Doug & VyAnn Grant

Katherine Nichols

Robin Rothbard

I also wish to thank Evan Swiech, cinematographer, for helping to create the Kickstarter video. We couldn't get those darn birds to cooperate, but the film turned out great anyway! Thank you for freezing out there in the snow with me in order to get great shots.

And a big thank you to Charlie Edwards, who was the voiceover on the video.
All those years in radio finally paid off, huh?

For

Anna Naomi

and

Audrey Grace

Table of Contents

CHAPTER 1

30 June, 10:42am

The only sound more piercing than the passengers' screams was the abrasive shrieking of the wheels against the rails. As the line of passenger train cars barreled into the station at the incredulous rate of over 200 miles per hour, the conductor pressed every button and pulled every lever available, but nothing could assuage the locomotive madness that steamrolled into the Rain Bahnhof in Bavaria, Germany.

In the next instant, the building looked like a war zone.

Casualty numbers escalated as the speeding tube came in contact with bystanders who were reading the daily news, with shop owners in the midst of making change for customers, and with businessmen discussing lucrative deals on their cell phones. Children stood wide-eyed, clasping their mothers' hands for only a moment; the sudden impact separated them before they had a chance to register what was happening.

Inside the train cars, men prayed and women screamed. Young passengers clung to the closest adults as if their larger bodies could shield them from death's fierce determination. Pockets of tourists, already confounded by the foreign language screaming over the intercom couldn't comprehend the scope of the emergency - except for the fact that the train should have slowed during its approach into the station instead of speeding up.

Frenzied panic ripped through the entire terminal. Chairs and benches were thrown into the air, kiosks were bandied about as if they were juggling balls, and papers sailed like turbulent whirlwinds of confetti. Pieces of jagged metal and steel sliced menacingly at everything in their way as if to make a dire point. Nuts and bolts shot out from the various cars, piercing through the hardest concrete as well as the softest skin. Glass shards stabbed, penetrated and ravaged bodies; cutting into, cutting through.

The destruction knew no rank, no age and no status. When the carnage was tallied up, the devastation was almost unprecedented. The people killed upon impact were believed to be the lucky ones; the others resembled the walking dead as they ambled about, existing somewhere in between this world and the next. These were the people who shuffled through the remains of the station looking for someone they knew, someone that might have survived.

The ones who had limbs torn from their bodies searched through mountains of wreckage for their lost body parts. Others, whose faces were now unrecognizable, crawled over piles of steaming carnage to comfort the ones that were worse off. A few simply lay where they had fallen, waiting for either an angel of mercy or a guardian of death.

When the emergency crews arrived, they expected a high number of casualties, but also assumed there would be a number of survivors who could easily be transported. Instead, they walked into an apocalyptic scenario that was unlike anything they had ever encountered. The shell-shocked wanderers that were ambulatory had begun ravaging the dead for their limbs, tearing off hunks of flesh and eating them.

The emergency responders tried to make sense of the chaos, attempting to triage the people that were still alive. A priest on the scene explained away the horrific behaviors by claiming that the injured didn't know what they were doing. They couldn't be held responsible for desecrating the bodies because they weren't in their right minds after such a monumental accident.

Local hospitals would be overwhelmed for several weeks. Exhausted doctors and nurses would be pushed to their limits; both mentally and psychologically. A disaster of this magnitude had not been seen before, especially one with a cannibalistic twist.

Engineers, investigators, and mechanics would be brought in to determine the cause of the catastrophe. Meetings would take place; men would be held accountable and then fired. A few distraught railway employees would end up taking their own lives out of misplaced guilt.

Yards upon yards of *Caution* tape would be wrapped around the small train station for months, giving the appearance that the building was a hideous gift to the people of Rain; a chilling reminder of the events that took place on that godforsaken day.

◆ ◆ ◆

The final body count from the accident totaled ninety-nine. The physical ills that the survivors had suffered eventually healed over time but their psychological states remained confounded. Not a single person who lived through the ordeal could recall anything that happened after the initial impact. Every psychiatrist, doctor, nurse, and family member had been told the same thing by the patients: *the train crashed as it entered the station house and the next thing they remembered was waking up in the hospital.* Even after being pointedly questioned by the authorities regarding the consumption of the dead, no one had an answer. Such inquires were met with blank stares.

The municipalities in the small towns surrounding Rain bickered for a month over what to do with the now defunct train station. After three months, a heroic attempt was made to renovate the structure in order to provide a secondary station for tourists traveling in the remote area, but it was eventually scrapped. The building and the platform were truly beyond repair. While some early cosmetic fixes proved successful and initially motivated the workers, rebuilding the foundation was too complex. It was like starting from scratch, trying to rebuild Frankenstein's monster from discarded shards of bone and mismatched swathes of skin.

The workers had been able to modify the building enough for it to appear functional, but ultimately the costs were too high. During the second phase of the reconstruction, workmen kept unearthing body parts and remains. Everyone involved became too discouraged to continue and all progress came to a halt. Discussions eventually led to the decision to tear down the entire structure in order to create some sort of memorial, but those were plans for sometime in the future. There had already been too much time and effort and emotion wrapped up in the project. For now, everyone needed time away, time to heal.

The Rain Bahnhof remained standing; a monument to tragedy and death. A concrete symbol of what can happen when man's futile attempt to make the world go *faster* backfires.

◆ ◆ ◆

10 July – Headline from the Rain, Germany Gazette

A cracked wheel and a faulty break system caused the ICE (intercity express) to derail upon arrival at the Rain Bahnhof on 30 June. Ninety-nine people were killed and many others maimed during the accident. No charges are being filed at this time.

CHAPTER 2

1 December, 17:50 (5:50pm)

Gary Wolf lifted two grey suitcases up by their leather handles and looked back toward his wife. He watched as she fussed with her hair in front of the hotel's lobby mirror. He rolled his eyes. If there was one thing Gary had learned during their eight day belated honeymoon trip in Germany, it was that the German people are a *punctual* people. A train which is scheduled for an 18:08 departure will be leaving at precisely 18:08. The doors will shut and the wheels will start to roll. Grace Wolf was apparently still living on Bloomington, Illinois time, where ten minutes either way wouldn't make much of a difference.

He verbally nudged her, hoping she would take the hint. Luckily for him, she did. Grace turned, nodded, and picked up her own suitcase and matching carry-on. She caught up to him right before he entered the turnstile doors, just in time for his not-so-subtle rebuke.

"Grace, we're going to miss our train and I don't think I have to remind you how bad that would be. It's the last one leaving today for the airport and if we don't make it, our plane tickets aren't going to be worth shit."

"We're not going to miss it just because I stopped to fix my hair."

"Well, we still have about four blocks to walk according to my directions. That doesn't leave us with much time to get tickets and figure out where we need to be."

"Why can't we just take a cab?"

"It's quicker this way. I'll show you on the map once we get there. It's a straight shot down Oberlander until we turn onto Marzplatz. The station is on the corner of Marzplatz and Nefflerstrasse. It sounds complicated but it's not. Anyway, a cab would cost extra and the walk will do us some good. Move around now while you can because we're going to be sitting on a plane for the next nine hours."

Grace nodded as she toddled after her husband. Her 5'3 frame hefting 200 pounds struggled to keep up with her lean and fit 5'11, 170 pound spouse. He was the healthy one in the family, there was no doubt about that. His morning routine started at 5:15am. He was dressed and out the door for a five mile run before the clock hit 5:30. A little over half an hour later, he'd arrive home in time to shower and shave before heading to the office by eight. All this would take place before Grace opened a single sleepy eye; a delicious advantage of garnering a sizable monthly check from a court-appointed maintenance judgment.

The mismatched pair turned the corner and headed for a building topped with red letters which spelled *Bahnhof*. The structure was somewhat small in comparison to the train station in Normal, Illinois, the town adjacent to Bloomington.

From the outside and in the dark, the shape of the building reminded Grace of a worm - - a long cement tube with a mouth in the front (the entrance) on one end, and an anus, where the trains entered and exited, on the other. They approached its cold, metallic lips.

Grace was startled by a broken and misshapen gargoyle that had been carved into an abutment where the handrail and the door to the entrance met. Gary smirked as he heard her gasp.

They stepped carefully, maneuvering between the drifts of snow and chunks of ice that coated much of the stairway. Grace grunted up each step as she dragged her overstuffed suitcase over each slippery stair. Her husband was already at the door, bags perched next to him, trying to read a crinkled, yellow sign.

"It's locked," Gary called out from the top of the stairway.

"Did you try the door next to it?"

"Of course I did. There's a sign here, but hell if I know what it says."

"Wait a minute. I have the German dictionary in my purse. Let me get up there an' I'll look up the words."

"Forget it. We don't have time. We still gotta get the tickets and according to my phone, we've got about ten minutes before the train pulls away."

He picked up his suitcases and trotted down to where Grace was standing.

"Here, watch these and I'll see if I can find another way in."

Grace nodded. She dipped her hand into her oversized purse, blindly rummaging around, feeling for the German to English pocket dictionary. She made her way up the steps, sans suitcases, and began to translate.

"*Geschlossen*...," she mumbled, thumbing through the thin, glossy pages. "Here we go. It means *closed*."

"Grace," Gary yelled. "Over here. There's a side door that I think we can squeeze through."

He ran toward her, thumb pointing over his shoulder behind him.

"I think we can get in that way. Grab your stuff and let's go." He lifted his own suitcases and paused, hoping she would follow suit.

She pointed at the sign.

"This sign says 'closed'. I looked it up."

"Of course it does. Come on, we don't have much time."

◆ ◆ ◆

Squeezing through the side door was trickier than Gary imagined. It wouldn't open all the way, but by using his foot, a suitcase and a little muscle, he was able to pry it wide enough for him and his wife to wedge themselves and their baggage through.

Once inside the station's belly, the contrariness of the building's interior in relation to the previous station became very apparent to Grace. When they arrived eight days earlier, their Lufthansa flight had delivered them to the northern part of the country, near Berlin. The airport was a bustling hub of activity, with all the modern conveniences any traveler might desire. A literal cavalcade of life. Shop owners hawking pretzels, a wide array of newspapers from numerous countries in languages she had never seen, people coming and going at all speeds in every direction. It seemed like everyone was plugged into one device or another. Men and women chatted on their cell phones while oblivious youngsters bounced through the terminal to their own soundtrack through the courtesy of their headphones.

This terminal was very different.

The ceiling and walls were part brick, part cement, and part metalwork; none of which looked finished. The other station, the one in Berlin, reminded Grace of Bloomington's Ewing Manor, a residence that was built in the late 1920's for Mr. and Mrs. Davis Ewing after they had traveled around the world. While that was a beautiful and well-preserved structure, a place that Grace enjoyed visiting, *this* station's architectural anatomy left her feeling disoriented and unwelcome.

As she continued to eye the uncomfortable surroundings, Gary remained vigilant. The station *was* rather tube-like. They had entered from an emergency exit on one side of the worm, just past the main entrance. They would have to head toward the bowels, the place where the single track entered and exited the building to get to their train. A clock, which hung in the middle of the long corridor, caught Gary's eye.

"Ten after six? Holy shit! We've got five minutes to get our asses on that train."

Grace didn't move. For some unknown reason, she suddenly felt claustrophobic. She wanted to curl up in a fetal position, throw a blanket over her head, and cower in the darkness. For all she cared at that moment, Gary could get on the train, head to the airport and leave the continent without her. She felt a sense of dread creep through the terminal and envelop her with its elongated tentacles, crushing the air out of her lungs. Her mousey brown hair hung in rivulets around her sweaty face; another contradictory experience in her life, given the puffy winter coat, hat, and scarf she wore.

Gary was not amused.

"Grace, *come on*. Let's *go*."

"I'll wait here with the luggage," she choked. A tear rolled down her sweaty cheek.

"Really? You're gonna pull this little girl pouty shit *now*? Look, we don't have time to mess around."

"There's something wrong with this place. I don't think we should be in here."

"The only thing wrong is that we're going to miss our only train to the airport," he said as he dropped one of his bags and grabbed his wife's hand in an attempt to pull her forward. "Get over here. We can argue about whatever you want after we board. Grab your stuff and let's move."

Gary let her hand go, picked up his bags and jogged down the dimly-lit corridor toward the track as Grace reluctantly trudged after him. On the way, they passed a bakery, a newsstand, and a couple of empty kiosks which once held touristy gifts like miniature beer steins and pen knives emblazoned with images of castles. There was also a clock shop and a clothing store, but there was no time left for window shopping.

As they approached the track, they saw a single train protruding from the tunnel – an engine with two passenger cars protruding from the middle of the worm's anus. A few wooden benches were situated on one side and two ticket machines stood against the far wall next to the tunnel. Not a single poster or sign or advertisement – the usual things one might see in a train station or airport – graced the area. The walls were bare, gray, and dusty. The emergency lights in the corners of the lobby, the only bright spots in the building, made Grace shudder.

"I can't."

Gary stopped in mid-step and turned to face his wife.

"What can't you do?"

She stopped next to one of the benches that faced the train and set her bags down.

"Didn't you notice something weird as we were running down the hall? Gary, we're the only people in the whole building."

His face contorted as if it had been slapped. Having been in such a blinding rush to get to their train, it never dawned on him until that moment that there were no other commuters, no shop owners, no children running about. He spun around comically, first to his left, then his right. He cupped his hands around his mouth and shouted.

"*Hello! Anybody here? Hello?*"

No answer.

"Shit."

"What? What is it?" Grace asked.

"We...we might be in the wrong station," Gary sputtered, patting his coat pockets for their itinerary. He found the folded sheet in the back pocket of his jeans. He followed his finger with his eyes, frantically searching for the departure information.

"Dammit! Where...what's this place called? Jesus, we're supposed to be in *Bogen*. I saw this place when we got to our hotel and I just figured...oh, man. We'll never make it. Our train's probably leaving as we speak. *How could I be so stupid?*"

He crumpled up the offending paper, threw it on the floor and kicked at an innocent bench. The echo reverberated off the stark walls.

"Well, let's just go to Bogen. We should be able to catch *some* train, even if we have to leave tomorrow."

Gary ran his hands through his hair. A cowlick stood at attention near the back of his head.

"Yeah, okay. Grab your stuff. We can probably *exit* through the front doors, even though they're locked from the outside."

Grace nodded. She was at least three paces behind Gary the whole way as she followed him back to the mouth of the station, suitcase wheels spinning wildly.

CHAPTER 3

1 December, 12:30pm

Four thousand, five hundred and eighty one miles away, Sarah and Mike Waverly pulled in to the Olive Garden's parking lot from Veterans Parkway in Bloomington, Illinois. Snow had fallen throughout the early part of the morning, making the drive from their house to the restaurant a slushy one. Still, living on the east side of town made the trip to the Italian eatery a little more palatable, taking less time than it would have if they had driven from the far side of Normal. Although the central Illinois twin cities, Bloomington-Normal, butted up against one another, it could easily take twenty-odd minutes to get from one end of town to the other; traffic and weather notwithstanding.

A friendly blonde hostess sat the couple at a booth tucked away in a back nook near a window overlooking a side parking lot. Within a few minutes, a young waiter took their drink orders, shared the day's specials, and left them alone to peruse the new winter menu.

Mike and his wife, Sarah, were both realtors and worked in the same office as Gary for the past ten years, and had become neighbors over the past two. Mike and Gary were best friends since their college days. When Sarah married Mike, she befriended Gary rather easily. It was Grace who had always been the odd wheel out.

Two years ago, when Gary began seeing Grace, both Sarah and Mike held their collective tongues. The whirlwind romance between their friend and this dowdy woman was disconcerting to say the least. It wasn't until the relationship took a serious turn that they felt it was time to intervene. Almost three months after their first date, Gary made the official announcement during a barbeque cookout at their house.

"Guys, I'm getting married."

"What?" Mike said. "Are you kidding me? That's great, man. Who's the lucky lady?"

Gary smiled. "Grace, of course. Who'd ya think? We're gonna make it short and sweet. Head over to the courthouse, hand over a hundred and fifty bucks and sign the papers. Nothing fancy. But I'd sure love it if you guys were there. You know, for support, to be witnesses. What do ya say?"

"Oh, honey," Sarah said, "we'd do anything for you, you know that. But…," she hesitated and glanced at Mike. "You haven't known her very long, have you? What's it been, like three months? Four at the most?"

He grinned and rubbed the back of his neck with his hand.

"Yeah, yeah, I know. It's kind of a quick thing. But, I've never been one for all that pomp and circumstance shit. I just want to make it legal. Quick and to the point."

"If *you're* happy, *we're* happy, right Sar'?" Mike added.

"Why rush into this, Gary? I have to say, I've never pegged you for a hurry-to-the-alter kind of guy," Sarah said, continuing to look to her husband for support.

"Well, I'm no spring chicken anymore," Gary said, winking at Mike.

"I wouldn't say that, man. I don't think being forty is over the hill just yet. Hell, we both passed that little mile-marker a couple of years ago. Didn't we, dear?"

Sarah made a face and took a drink from her margarita.

"Yeah, don't remind me."

"That was some blowout, you guys," Gary said, sipping on his beer. "Memorable."

"Look, Gary. If she's really the one, that's great. We just don't want to see you rush into anything, you know what I mean? There's so many young and upbeat people out there. I-I just don't know if she's, uh, your contemporary."

"Ugh, just say it, dear," Sarah bemoaned. "Isn't Grace a little conservative and old-fashioned for your taste? I mean, the woman dresses like a grandma for Chrissake and she's *our* age. She doesn't drink, which is fine, but she doesn't like to go anywhere at all. And she practically falls apart when she hears a swear word. I've seen some of the other women you've dated in the past and they were *nothing* like *her*. What's the big attraction?"

Gary swirled the remaining beer around in his glass before chugging the rest in one swallow. A tiny burp bubbled past his lips. He wiped his mouth with a napkin.

"Let's just call it a wise financial move on my part, okay?"

◆ ◆ ◆

Without realizing what he had done, he looked down to find the fork tines bent backward toward the handle. His brow furrowed and his mouth strained downward at each corner. He tried to hide the utensil underneath his menu.

"What's the matter, dear? Rethinking your drink order? You've always loved their dirty martinis here."

Her questions dragged him back into the moment.

"Oh, uh, no. Sorry. My mind just wandered away for a minute."

"Well, I hope it comes back before our waiter does. Do you know what you're having? You barely looked at the menu. And…oh, Mike, you better ask for another fork. Are you sure you're okay?"

"No, I'm good. I was just thinking about Gary."

"Did you hear from him? We're still picking them up at the airport later tonight, right?"

"Yeah, we're still on as far as I know. But, no, I didn't hear anything else from him."

"Then what are you so worried about? Something must be eating at you…enough to make you destroy cutlery."

She laid her menu down and reached for his hands. Mike turned his head and stared out the window. He saw an elderly man being helped into a car by an older lady he assumed was the man's wife. She shut his door, walked around the front of the car, scooted into the driver's seat and started the engine. Mike continued to watch as the woman helped the man buckle his seat belt and adjust the heater vents. Once he appeared to be comfortable, she handed him a pair of sunglasses and patted him on the shoulder. In the next moment, she pulled a gun out of her purse and shot him through his left temple, splattering his head across the passenger door and window.

"*Dear?*"

Mike jumped at the sound of his wife's voice at the same time he witnessed the shooting. He blinked again and looked out the window. The old man was fine. There was no blood; no gun had been fired. The woman backed the car out of the parking lot while the two chatted and laughed, obviously enjoying each other's company.

"Mike?"

"Grace."

"What about Grace?"

"I-I was thinking...about her."

Sarah rolled her eyes and let go of Mike's hands.

"I thought you said you were thinking about Gary. Why is she on your mind? We'll be seeing her later tonight and that's soon enough as far as I'm concerned."

Mike broke a buttery breadstick in half. He bit the end of it and chewed while Sarah continued. He shifted in his seat and turned away from the window. When the waiter brought his drink, Mike asked him to take it away.

"I, uh, I'll pay for it. I just don't feel much like alcohol right now. Can you bring me a Diet Coke instead?"

The waiter complied and removed the glass from the table.

"Dear, you don't look so hot all of a sudden. Would you rather go home right now?"

He shook his head and took another bite of bread.

"Mm, no. I...I'm okay. I'm just not in the drinking mood. Now, what were you saying before? Something about Grace?"

"I don't like her," Sarah snapped. "She's a prude and she's judgmental, especially when it comes to us. Gary is completely the opposite."

As Mike picked up another breadstick, he finally gave in to the unsettling magnetic pull that kept drawing his attention to the window. He watched as a lone snowflake came to rest on a dead leaf. He tried to turn aside from the outside world, but found it impossible to look away.

"I guess that's why I'm worried."

CHAPTER 4

"C*an't you push any harder?"*

Gary released the metal handle and kicked at the door in one swift motion.

"G'damn fucking thing. It won't budge," he scoffed, sloppily kicking at it a second and third time.

"What about trying the side door? You know, where we came in at?"

"Yeah. Yeah, let's try that."

Once again, Grace toddled after Gary, her small feet scuttling across the cement floor, trying to keep up with her husband's quick pace. She glanced up toward the ceiling; the only lights guiding their way were the emergency backups. The few scant windows which graced the top of the wall along the corridor and the lobby area where the train was were of no help. Sunset has long passed.

"Your hair is sticking up," Grace said.

He sighed, paused for a moment and swept his hand over the back of his head. The cowlick retreated.

"It's not like we have a lot of time here, Grace," he muttered under his breath. She didn't hear his retort.

When they got to the side door, Grace stood a few feet away, dutifully guarding their belongings while Gary attempted to open the emergency exit. He removed his gloves in order to get a better grip on the handle and leaned hard into the push. When it wouldn't budge, he quickly studied the frame, the lock and the glass, trying to find a weak spot which would allow some maneuverability. He motioned for Grace to help. Between the two of them, they managed to work up a sweat and a growing frustration, but no movement from the door itself.

Gary released the metal handle along with a string of expletives. He wanted to kick the door, but refrained. He didn't need a legful of glass shards to deal with on top of everything else.

"Now what?" Grace asked, examining her reddened hands.

"Plan B. Whatever the hell that is."

◆ ◆ ◆

Grace hunkered down on one of the wooden benches and surrounded herself with their luggage. She dug a paperback out from the bottom of her carry-on bag and thumbed through the pages. A number of older dog ears silently saluted her as she flipped through the cozy mystery to find her current place in the book. Gary watched as his wife pretended to get comfortable. He knew better.

"It shouldn't take me long to find another exit around here. There's nothing to worry about. The place doesn't look that big; just one long tube."

"Very wormlike," she said, holding her book in her lap.

"Yeah, well, I can scout this worm out a lot faster without having to drag a bunch of suitcases around. Stay here and I'll be back in no time, alright?"

Grace nodded. She wanted to tell him to be careful, but thought better of it. He was only walking down a corridor. *What could possibly be dangerous about that?* Her eyes never left him; his confident stride and determined outlook gave her some comfort. He had always been able to radiate aplomb, a quality which first attracted her to Gary.

Two and a half years ago, after her divorce was finalized, Grace found herself in a free-fall. She didn't have many friends, her parents had already passed on, and she was an only child. She knew of a few distant relatives who lived around the St. Louis area, over three hours away, but she couldn't imagine leaving her church. Somehow, she would have to make do and stay in Bloomington-Normal; she just wasn't sure how at that point.

The weekend after her divorce papers were finalized, Grace was in Schnucks grocery and had picked up the latest Home Shopper magazine. Enter Gary Wolf, real estate workaholic, always on the lookout for a potential client. When he sidled up beside her in the cereal aisle, he noticed the publication lying in her cart.

"Looking for a home?"

Grace turned to face the curious stranger.

"Well, I guess I am. Just got the papers yesterday."

"Ma'am?"

"Divorce papers. We have to sell the house. It was in the decree."

That was all Gary needed to hear. After playing the role of concerned and empathetic listener, he managed to charm and persuade her into having dinner with him that evening, letting her take the lead and direct the conversation. It wasn't much of a surprise to him that the primary topic leaned heavily on the recent divorce.

"So," Gary took a long drink of water, "Ed was never formally charged with anything?"

"No," Grace sighed, poking at an innocent tortellini. "But *I* saw. I know what he did 'cause I lived with him. There were at least a hundred pictures of little kids on that computer. Well, not little. More like twelve, thirteen…I don't know. I just know that I couldn't live like that."

"So you couldn't prove it. To a lawyer, I mean."

She shook her head and stabbed her fork into a wayward pasta shell.

"Everything disappeared after I confronted him with it. Like it was never there in the first place. But he knew. *He* knew that *I* knew and that's why he agreed to a divorce and to pay me monthly alimony, even if I get married again. Ed couldn't handle anyone suspecting him for a second. You can imagine what would happen if something like that ever got out. Just the idea that somebody might be into that sort of thing makes people sick."

"Yeah, yeah," Gary said. He twirled some spaghetti onto his fork. "Nothing good can come out of a situation like that…for you *or* for him. But that's why you don't have to work anymore?"

Grace smiled and filled her mouth with pasta pillows.

"Yep."

"That must be a heck of a maintenance settlement, if I may say."

"Five thousand every month. Free and clear. He makes a pretty high six-figure salary. He can afford it."

Gary's face lit up. *Sixty-thousand a year with no taxes to report.* He reached across the table and took her hands in his. A smile swept across his face. His heart was racing. In a good year, he was lucky if he broke 42K.

"Grace, I'm having such a wonderful time this evening. May I call on you again soon?"

It had taken only three and a half months for Gary's charm, wit and unyielding attention to win her over. Naturally, Gary took care of finding them the perfect home, on the same street as his best friend, Mike. He also made sure that all the papers were in Grace's name *only*. She was, after all, footing the bill.

◆ ◆ ◆

Grace opened her book, The Darkened Stairwell: The Mystery of a Notorious Bannister, to page 119 and tried to pick up where she last left off, but found it almost impossible to focus. She thought she heard Gary pounding against the walls and knocking on store windows. More than anything, she felt torn. She had promised to stay with the luggage but she ached to chase after him in order to soothe her own fears. Either decision came with its own consequence, but ultimately, she stuck to her word and babysat their belongings.

She took in a long, deep breath and let it out slowly. *No*, she told herself. *It's best to sit here and read; take your mind off of things while you wait.* Grace lowered her eyes to the page. The words were bleeding.

She gasped, jumped from the bench and flung the paperback high into the air. Covering her mouth with her trembling hands, she felt tears well up in her eyes, but blinked them away.

The thought of pushing the door with the metal bar ran across her mind. Maybe she had inadvertently cut herself in the attempt. She looked at her hands, expecting them to be spotted with crimson, but there was nothing streaked across her pink flesh. Not a drop.

The novel lay, sprawled open on the cold, dirty floor like an old hooker waiting to be picked up from a shady alley. With her hands shaking and her body still trembling, Grace scurried over and snatched it up, forcing the pages closed. She took a deep breath and let it out through puffed up cheeks, but didn't dare open the book again. *Not until Gary comes back,* she told herself. *Nothing bad will happen as long as he's here with me.*

She set the book on the bench, folded her hands in her lap and sat facing the engine, waiting silently for her knight in blue jeans to rescue her from herself.

CHAPTER 5

13 November, 10:00am

Community leaders from the Rain municipality as well as other surrounding areas, all of whom were part of the larger Straubing-Bogen district, gathered in a large meeting room on the second floor of a government building in the town of Bogen. It was a beautiful area, tucked away between the southern slopes of the Bavarian Forest and the Danube River. The contrast between the picturesque surroundings and the reason for the meeting was not lost on those in attendance. From the outset, there was a pall over the proceedings. Pieter Hinter, the Zoning Supervisor, was in charge and presided over the project at hand.

"Johanna, please, if you would read the minutes from our last meeting, yes?"

"The entire transcript?"

"No. Just the portion that's relevant for today's meeting."

"Of course."

"Regarding the decision to raze the Rain Bahnhof – the committee unanimously voted to pass with a vote of eleven to zero. The secondary point, to install a memorial in its place, was also passed unanimously by a vote of eleven to zero.

The date for demolition of the Rain Bahnhof has been tentatively scheduled to take place on 2 December at approximately 0900 hours. Surrounding businesses and private homes will be alerted to possible debris and noise issues pertaining to the activity. The district has agreed to commission engineers and workers from Rain as well as others from the surrounding municipalities."

A dead silence cloaked the stark white room.

"Continue please, Johanna."

"There is nothing more, sir. The minutes end there."

Pieter Hinter stared at the woman as if she held a tantalizing secret. She shook her head as if to negate his pensive expression.

"There was nothing else, Mr. Hinter."

He blinked and cleared his throat. All eyes were on him.

"It looks as though we still have much work to do then, gentlemen. Since the deconstruction is scheduled for 2 December, there isn't much time to finalize our plans."

CHAPTER 6

Gary Wolf searched through the faintly lit corridor for any possible nook or cranny where a hidden exit, an employee entrance or a land line telephone might hide. The few storefronts he had already passed were more than just empty; they were decimated. Broken glass, metal shards and random garbage littered what was left of the entryways. Upon closer investigation, the only certainty he could determine were varying shades of darkness, illuminated by the glint of light from his cell phone. Gloom and decay were plentiful here.

The few small windows set high along the walls in the area were of no help, so Gary held his phone out in front of him like a beacon in a storm. He felt awkward about calling out, yet managed to shout a friendly *hello* into one or two of the shop doorways. He wasn't surprised by the lack of response.

As he neared the front of the building, the maw of the worm, he noticed the bakery to his left. This particular storefront caught his attention because the windows were still intact and the door frame looked as solid as anything he had seen at

Eastland Mall in Bloomington. He went up to the glass front, pressed his phone against the window and peered in to get a better look.

The main counter was covered with a blue and white gingham print cloth. In the center, a perfect pyramid of muffins were stacked at least a foot high. To their right was a basket brimming with cookies, tiny cakes and other pastries. As he moved the light back and forth, he saw what appeared to be boxes of pies stacked up in rows.

From where he stood and how he felt, everything about this glorious find was a godsend. Gary hadn't realized just how hungry he was until he laid eyes on the spread before him. As his stomach growled, he realized he had begun to salivate. He had to get into that shop by any means possible. He tucked his phone into his pocket and tried the door. When it wouldn't cooperate, he shoved his body hard against the entrance until the heavy door gave way. Once inside, he stood motionless, taking in the delectable aromas of freshly baked breads and warm sugar cookies.

He clicked the flashlight back on and methodically moved the beam around the shop.

"Hello? Anybody here?"

The shelves behind the counter were bare with the exception of a paper box, a bent cup lid, and an empty cookie tray. A broken light fixture hung from the middle of the ceiling. It appeared to have had a working fan at one time. Now, two of the blades dangled precariously by shredded cords, while the other two stuck out at unnatural angles. All four were covered in grit.

A large glass fixture, the showcase where specials of the day would have been beautifully displayed for hungry customers, now lay in pieces scattered across the floor.

The muffins and pastries that initially called to him from the window came into his line of sight. He put a hand against his stomach to quell the audible rumbling.

"Better find a phone first," he mumbled, eyeing the treats.

Easing his way between random boards and pieces of glass, Gary navigated through the chaos to the back of the shop. He moved his light from surface to surface, straining in the shadowy confines in order to see as much as he could.

"There's nothing *here* that'll help. Fuck."

Stepping around and over the dusty debris, Gary closed in on the muffins and their tasty friends. He laid the phone on the counter, wiped his hands on his pants, and began shoveling one muffin after another into his mouth. Chewing just enough to force a swallow, he downed at least six before he could stop himself. He eyed the pies and lifted one of the lids. He paused for a moment before closing it.

"No, better not," he smirked and wiped his face with his coat sleeve.

He tinkered with the idea of bringing a pie back for Grace, but dismissed the thought with a snort. *Why encourage that kind of behavior? It's not like she doesn't eat enough garbage at home.* He turned his phone to the doorway and left the shop empty-handed.

He tried another door; a clothier. It gave way easier than he expected. With a single grunt and a gentle push, he found himself in the entryway. This store appeared to be in the same state of upheaval as the bakery. The few remaining empty racks were toppled over; bent wire hangers had been scattered about. Among the disarray was a lone pair of pants which had been crumpled into a ball, a couple of leather belts coiled up like sleeping snakes, and a random assortment of zippers and buttons. The floor was covered with a poorly cut carpet remnant.

A thin plastic cable also ran along the floor. Gary tracked it with his light. It traveled up the back wall and disappeared behind a counter. He stumbled around the fallen furniture to follow its path.

"There's gotta be a phone on the end of this thing."

He got on his hands and knees and pulled the line toward him. He started slowly, wrapping the thin plastic tube around his arm, but the longer it took, the faster he began to pull. A minute turned into two, then three. Hand over hand, yanking on the cord as quickly and furiously as he could, the whole scenario was beginning to feel like some awful prank. *Until something on the other end pulled back.*

The shock of the resistance startled him. Cautiously, he tugged at the line and found there was more to give. Sweat beaded around his hairline and dripped down his back. Gary tore at the cord with a ferocity that was unstoppable. The pile of cable was growing into a mountainous heap.

"Where's the *end* of this freakin' thing?"

The coil was now towering over him as he crouched on the floor behind the back counter. The more he pulled, the more frustrated he became. His hands were flying, faster and faster, trying to get to the end of this madness.

"Where's the fucking phone?"

Almost on cue, the cord snapped in two. The abrupt halt sent Gary tumbling backwards into the tangled weave of cable, knocking his own phone from its position on the counter, taking away what little light he had. In the process, the faceplate broke and shattered into a glass web.

"G'dammit!"

He let go of the busted cord and blindly felt around the floor for his phone. When his hand made contact, he breathed a sigh of relief. Gary pressed a button and heard a beep. The device whirred back to life.

"Thank God. At least *you* still work, you damn piece of shit," he chuckled.

He untangled himself from the wiry mess and brushed off the dust and debris from his clothes. As he was checking for his wallet, there was a rustling sound near the front of the store.

"Hello?"

Within seconds, the noise moved considerably closer to him.

Gary held his phone out, trying to get the flashlight app to work but it wasn't cooperating.

"Are you the owner here? Sorry, I can't see you, my phone...,"

The shuffling noise was very close now, within an arm's distance. Gary alternated between poking at buttons on the phone and shaking it.

"I-I'm sorry, I can't...get this...,"

In the next moment, Gary felt hot breath on his face. Instinctively, he recoiled, but was literally caught between the wall behind him and the counter and piles of cord in front of him.

"Who – who...?"

With a final Hail Mary slap on the back of his phone, the light blinked on. He held the device out to see who had been with him in the dark, watching as he pulled phone cord into a fruitless electrical heap. Who had the nerve to approach him, to spy on him, to get close enough to *breathe on him?*

Two mannequins dressed in dirndls and lederhosen stared at Gary with lidless eyes; their mouths hung partially open as if to question the motive of their uninvited visitor. The man and the woman were less than two feet away, close enough for Gary to see that their clothes were streaked with blood and their hands held clumps of human hair.

Gary gasped and futilely threw himself back against the wall. There wasn't enough space to get away from these intruders. *There couldn't possibly be enough* as far as he was concerned.

The mannequins let out a long, asthmatic, acrid sigh before collapsing backwards on to the floor.

Gary didn't move. He wasn't sure of what he saw; *if* he really saw anything at all. He rubbed his neck and then his eyes. He drew a hand through his hair. Keeping the light on the two fallen interlopers, he clumsily climbed over the counter that had blocked his initial escape. Now, free from all manner of cable piles and store furniture, he timidly approached the mannequins for a better look. He felt nauseous, but forced himself to do it. He held the phone out and studied their faces.

They were so…*lifelike?* No, that wasn't it.

They were so *death*like.

CHAPTER 7

Mike handed the bill and his MasterCard over to the waiter who had brought Sarah a handful of extra mints after hearing her exclaim how much she loved them. Mike stood, rubbing his legs to encourage the blood flow back into them. He stretched his arms upward, high enough to touch the top of the archway and yawned. Sarah watched his display.

"Oh, Mike. I was hoping we could run over to the mall real quick. Would you mind?"

He yawned again, wider this time.

"Do we have to?" He stretched again and took his coat from the bench. "I was hoping to get in a quick nap. I have a feeling we'll be up pretty late tonight an' I have to be in the office early tomorrow morning."

Sarah pouted just as the waiter returned with Mike's card. The two men exchanged glances and the smallest of smiles. The young man thanked them for coming in and wished them a pleasant afternoon.

"Okay, Sar'. But let's not make a whole day of it, huh?"

Sarah got up and hugged her husband.

"Thanks, hon. I promise – we'll be in and out in ten minutes."

◆ ◆ ◆

The Waverleys pulled into the Eastland Mall parking lot and secured a close spot near the north side door near Bergner's department store. Arm in arm, they walked through the entrance and were instantly greeted by strains of Joy to the World, oversized ornaments, and giant cardboard snowflakes. A couple of kids ran past in search of Santa and his reindeer, the seasonal picture-taking opportunity set up in one of the atriums.

"I wanted to get a little something for Gary. You know, sort of a homecoming present. How about one of those candles from White Barn? They smell so good, don't they? They make you want to take a bite out of them."

Mike laughed. He knew exactly what she meant. Whatever they did to make the gingerbread or peppermint or his personal favorite, the vanilla cream, smell like *that*, was worth every penny. Humming along with the overhead Muzak, he unhooked his arm from hers, took her by the hand and strolled toward their destination. Sarah stopped as they turned the corner. The Calendar Kiosk was abuzz with activity.

"Do you think I'm wrong?"

"What...about getting candles? You're thinking a calendar might be better? It looks like the place to be, don't you think?" Mike said.

"No, I don't mean about that. I mean about Grace."

"What are you talking about?"

"Well…," she hesitated.

They continued to walk through a maze of shoppers until they arrived at Bath and Body Works. A cardboard peppermint stick holding an array of shower poufs smiled down on them.

"Go on, Sar'. What about Grace?"

"Well, it's just that, you *do* spend an awful lot of time with Gary. Maybe Grace has a right to feel jealous."

Mike turned to face his wife amidst the holiday mall chaos bustling around them. He took both of her hands in his and laid them against his chest.

"The three of us work together in the same office. How can we *not* spend all of our days together? Add in conferences and our real estate classes and prep work. Hell, *we* should have been the ones on the honeymoon with him, not *her*!"

Sarah laughed. Mike smiled and hugged her.

"I still don't like her," she said.

"I'm not a big fan, either, but for Gary's sake…sometimes you gotta go along to get along, you know what I mean?"

She nodded. They entered the store and browsed through the holiday offerings along with the throngs of other people hoping to find a deal. Once they agreed on a large vanilla scented candle surrounded by a wreath of fake holly berries, they paid, left and headed back to their car.

Mike clicked the key fob as they approached their vehicle and the doors clicked open. Sarah got in first and placed their purchase in the back seat. The handle of the bag caught on an umbrella that had already taken up residence and caused the contents to spill onto the leather seat. The protective tissue paper floated to the floor of the car.

Mike had just opened the driver-side door with the intention of getting in, but the movement from the back seat caught his eye. He stopped dead cold. A shiver raced through his body and a wave of nausea washed over him. *What was he seeing?* A severed head lolled back and forth on the seat behind his wife. Its eyes were closed but its gaping mouth was distortedly open as if in mid-scream.

He covered his face with his hands and shook his head.

"Mike, hon? You okay?"

Sarah leaned over into the driver's seat and looked up at him.

"Are you sick?"

He lowered his hands and swallowed hard. The rear passenger seat once again carried an umbrella, an extra coat, a paper bag emblazoned with the White Barn logo and a cylindrical candle with a plastic wreath. There was no disembodied head hitching a ride.

"Mike?"

He scooted in behind the steering wheel and stared out the front window. Despite the temperature hovering in the teens, sweat rolled down his face.

"Maybe we *shouldn't* have gone to the mall. You don't look too well. Do you think it was something you ate?"

He turned to face her as he placed his hands on the dashboard.

"Yeah...let's say that's what it is and call it a day, huh?"

Mike turned the key, backed out of the parking space, and switched on the radio. He didn't feel much like talking, but he also didn't want to drive in silence. Instead, Mike found comfort in the strains of Bing Crosby's "White Christmas" as he drove home without ever looking in the rear view mirror.

CHAPTER 8

Grace had taken her phone out of her purse to check the clock. Gary had been gone for a while now, or at least what felt to *her* like a long time. The digital numbers blinked an eerie green: 7:05. She hadn't switched her phone to European time like Gary had. She didn't like telling time in *seventeen hundred* this or *twenty-one hundred* that. It made her uncomfortable.

From where she sat, the train's engine looked monstrous; a metallic machine that easily dwarfed her and divided what she thought of as the lobby area into two desolate halves. There might have been a few seats on the other side (she thought she remembered seeing them when they first arrived), but she wouldn't bet on it.

Waiting for her husband's grand return with an escape plan, *Plan B,* he called it, had been enough of a distraction. But he had been gone for over twenty-five minutes already and the station wasn't that big.

The lobby area was a little less dim than the rest of the station. Lit only by a handful of emergency lights, the entire building was shrouded in an unearthly hue. Everything looked grey and ghostly and sullen. What surprised Grace the most was the sheer silence of the place. It was almost deafening. She pulled her coat snug around her body and adjusted her hat. An uneasy chill bit into her, making her wonder how far the nearest bathroom was. Her nose began to run. She searched through her purse for a crumpled, unused tissue.

Between the cold air, the boredom of doing nothing, and the shadowy darkness, Grace's head lolled forward - once, twice, and by the third time, she had drifted off to sleep.

As she dreamed, she envisioned herself wandering through a huge, cavernous building. The ceiling was at least twenty feet high and the walls were as smooth and slick as a marble countertop. But the farther she walked, the narrower the walls became. She broke out into a loping run; her short stubby legs garnered her only a few inches with each step. In a frenzied panic, she lunged toward what appeared to be a doorway at the very end of the strangulating tunnel. On hands and knees, she crawled into the passage, cleared the tiny doorway, and found herself trapped inside of a cement coffin. Gary stood over her; the lid of the casket was in his hands and over his head.

"Thanks for the memories," Gary hissed and slammed the top down. She could hear nails being driven into the lid of the coffin as he and Kristy, his assistant from work, laughed. Kristy was egging him on to seal her up as quickly as possible.

"Finish the bitch off already," she chortled.

Grace slapped and kicked against the sides, screaming to be let out, pleading for Gary to stop.

When the final nail was pounded in, Grace gasped for air. She gagged and coughed and slammed her hands on the lid in front of her face. Though their voices were muted, she could still hear them discussing how they were going to spend all of her money now that she was out of the picture.

The more she screamed, the tighter the casket squeezed, crushing her from both sides, compressing her ribs against her lungs and internal organs. When the panels at both ends compressed inward, the force jammed her legs up into her torso. At the same time, the pressure was crushing the top of her head. The nightmare ended seconds later with a loud, grotesque pop as her head imploded.

Grace snapped awake with a dry, strangulated gasp. Sweat streamed down her face and her hands shook. As she alternated between rubbing her eyes and trying to catch her breath, Grace rocked herself back and forth. Her clothes were askew and her hat was hanging on the back of her head for dear life. The carry-on bag had been kicked underneath the seat during all the commotion and the contents of her purse were about two inches away from being splayed all over the ground.

As she bent down to collect her things, she looked down the dark body of the worm. She strained her eyes, willing them to focus long enough to see any hint of movement. She whispered, begging:

"Gary, where are you? What is taking you so long?"

◆ ◆ ◆

The shadow of a man appeared from the recess of the corridor, materializing into a welcome sight and an answer to Grace's prayers.

"Gary! Oh, thank God!"

Grace leaped off the floor and scurried toward her husband. She threw her arms around his neck and clung to him for dear life. He reached up to disengage himself from her suffocating embrace and took a seat on the bench.

"Jesus, Grace, calm down. I wasn't gone all that long."

"It felt long. It felt *too* long."

"Well, if you think *that* was a problem, you'll love this. I couldn't find another way out. I searched this entire station and couldn't even locate an employee exit."

"Oh, no. Are...are you *sure?*"

"I'm more than sure," Gary said. "It's just a weird freakin' place." As the words escaped his lips, he wished he hadn't spoken them. The last thing he wanted to do was to have to explain anything he saw...or *thought* he saw.

"What...what do you mean '*weird*'?"

Gary mentally kicked himself for bringing it up in the first place. He would have to pick and choose his words carefully. That is, if he wanted any semblance of calm for the rest of the evening. Grace was easily frightened and being worried about nothing was one of her favorite pastimes.

"Well, I had a look around the bakery and then went into the clothing store. They were close to each other, so, you know. It made sense."

"Sure. But that's not the weird part, is it?"

"No, Grace. That's not the weird part. I found a phone cord, or what I thought was a phone cord. I started pulling on it and it just kept coming out of the wall. I mean yards and yards of the stuff. I was sure I'd find a phone at some point, but the line just kept growing."

"So, what happened? Was there a phone on the end of it?"

"No. *That* was the weird part. It just broke off...right in my hand."

Grace sat down on the bench, looked at her husband, and shrugged.

"I dunno. I don't think that's so weird."

"Okay," Gary said, "I guess you're right...not so strange."

Grace shrugged again. She thought about her dream. *That* was weird.

"We need to go to Plan C if we're gonna get the hell out of here though. It's getting a little too late to keep screwing around."

"What's Plan C?"

"Call the police."

CHAPTER 9

Gary pulled his phone out of his pocket and looked down. When he saw the shattered screen, he cursed under his breath and put the device away. He held out his hand toward Grace.

"Here, let me have your phone."

"Why? What's the matter with yours?"

"The screen broke."

"How'd the screen break? It was fine when we left the hotel."

"I dropped it when I went looking for a landline. It was dark and it slipped out of my hands."

"Is it broken?"

"Well, it would be a lot easier if I could see the numbers I'm typing in. Let me just borrow yours, okay? It'll speed up the process."

"Here," she said, handing over her pink-skinned Samsung.

He took it, pressed 0, and listened for an operator. When nothing happened, he punched in 9-1-1 and waited. Still nothing.

"What the fuck? I'm not getting anything. How can you dial 9-1-1 and not get anybody?"

While Gary complained, Grace thumbed through her pocket-sized guide.

"Try 1-1-0. According to this, it should get you through to the police."

He nodded and dialed.

"It's ringing."

While he waited for an answer on the other end of the line, Gary paced around each bench, quietly pounding his fist against the top slat of wood. Grace watched him navigate for a moment before returning her attention to the index of her little book.

She knew Gary wasn't perfect; she wasn't *that* naïve when it came to her husband. She also had some inkling about what Sarah and Mike thought of her. She was an introvert and a homebody, but she was *content* to stay home and read her cozy mysteries or watch re-runs of re-runs on the Hallmark channel. She really didn't mind when Gary went out socializing without her. She preferred it, actually.

Real-estate agents like Gary were expected to attend a number of social events and business-oriented outings, both for his clients and his company. The only thing she didn't care for was his assistant, Kristy, the twenty-something single woman who wore the lowest cut blouses Grace had ever seen. And if her hemlines were any higher, she might as well just wear a belt around her waist for all that her skirt covered.

One time, when Grace had stopped by the office on the way to run an errand, she saw the way Kristy flirted with Gary; how she touched him on the arm and laughed at his horrible attempts at dry humor. During the company's summer picnic,

Kristy actually had the nerve to slap him on his rear end during a volleyball game. As far as Grace could tell, he didn't exactly discourage this kind of behavior.

She had wondered if there was something going on between them, but she didn't want to bring it up. For the first time since she had divorced Ed, she was finally feeling comfortable and safe again, and if that meant turning a blind eye to a little flirtatious behavior, then so be it.

◆ ◆ ◆

Ed Markum first met Grace when they were in junior high. They married right out of high school. He found work at their church and she found a job at Borders, a bookstore chain in Normal. They lived with his parents for the first few years in order to save up enough of their own money to purchase a small bungalow on the old west side of Bloomington.

After a few more quiet years had passed, Ed scored an interview with State Farm, a large insurance company with its headquarters located in the heart of Bloomington. It wasn't long before a number of promotions came his way, which provided the couple with an income they never imagined during their early years. They moved to a house on the east side of town, complete with a three-car garage, four bedrooms, three baths (one with a whirlpool tub) and a kitchen right out of House Beautiful. It was around this time that Grace discovered some questionable websites on Ed's personal computer. There was also the discovery of some very disturbing reading material hidden deep in his dresser.

Grace had no idea what the acronym NAMBLA stood for on the morning she was putting Ed's underwear away. She had reached into the bottom drawer of his bedroom dresser when she first made contact with the materials. The National Association of Man/Boy Love had published a newsletter and apparently Ed was on their mailing list.

She picked up the publication and flipped through the pages. There were stories and poems and pencil drawings that showed young boys and older men locked in a variety of embraces. On the back page was a list of suggestions about starting conversations with boys. There were also articles warning readers about what to say if you're caught in public with your young charge.

The discovery made her feel physically ill.

She buried the magazine back under the pile of plaid boxer shorts, slammed the drawer shut, and collapsed on their bed in a daze.

She didn't know whether to cry or vomit; perhaps both would make her feel better, though neither would make the truth go away. *How long had this been going on? Before the move? Before they were married? How could she not have known after this many years together?* She curled up into a fetal position on their king size bed, tears streaming down her face, hands quivering. What was she supposed to do? Ignore it? Confront him? Go to the police? Would she be seen as an accomplice if she *didn't* report him?

She stared at Ed's dresser, sick with revulsion, hating herself for not knowing what she should do. Having grown up in the church, she believed and trusted that she would always know the right decision to make if something like this ever happened. But she didn't.

After almost eighteen years of marriage, she was at a loss. Her head spun with scenario after scenario, none of which ended well for either of them. Hoping that her discovery was simply an unexplained fluke, she got off the bed, went into their den and turned on the computer. It didn't take long for her to locate Ed's *photography* folder. How did she not even *notice* it before?

She clicked on the little icon and the world she knew ended.

Picture after picture, screenshots of boys – in pools, on the beach, lifting weights, running in shorts. They all looked to be around twelve, maybe younger, maybe a year or two older. These were not men, though. Ed wasn't gay, she reasoned in her mind; although at this point she was almost hoping that he was – in comparison. *That*, she was certain, was something she could come to terms with…but not *this*.

She decided to confront him that evening after he came home from work. She didn't see any other real choice. Ignoring it might end up with him harming a child and that was not acceptable in any way, shape or form. Going to the police would be too public and open too many cans of worms. No, she would handle this herself. It would stay between the two of them; they would have to deal with the fallout on their own.

When Ed returned home that night from a long day at the office, she asked him to join her in their bedroom. Believing that he was in for some good old-fashioned husband-wife relations, he bounded up the stairs and leapt onto their bed.

"Grace, darling, this is rather forward of you…I mean, it's only Tuesday," he joked, unbuttoning his shirt.

She stepped further into the bedroom; a dour look strewn across her face. She turned the lights on and the overhead fan began to rotate.

"Lights *on* this time? You must have read one of those women's magazines. Sure, I'm game if you are, but I gotta say, this is really out of the box for you."

Without a word, she opened Ed's dresser drawer and fished her hand down to the bottom of the boxer brief pile. She grasped the publication in between her fingers and held it up in front of her face.

"And *this* is out of the box for *you? Or isn't* it?"

Ed's playful demeanor as well as his obvious physical expectations deflated. He stopped unbuttoning his shirt and swung his legs back over the side of the bed, scooting into a seated position. He placed his hands on his knees and lowered his head.

"How long?" Grace asked.

"You don't want to know."

"How long, Ed?"

"Grace, stop. Just…stop."

"You owe me that much. How long?"

"Long enough. Probably too long…,"

"Are you going to quit now?"

"No."

"Don't you love me, Ed? Don't you love me more than… than *this*?"

"That's another answer you don't want to know."

A week later, Grace's life was full of divorce lawyers, paperwork, and tearful nights. Because they agreed to keep the real reason for the split between themselves, their families, friends and co-workers were told that irreconcilable differences were to blame for the break-up.The divorce was amicable and quick. Ed took a transfer with his company to work in another state, but not before agreeing upon a private settlement with Grace, a secret deal on top of the court-appointed maintenance judgment she would receive. She would never have to work again; financially, she would be set for life. He would see to that.

He also told her that he loved her, but that she just wasn't enough for him.

◆ ◆ ◆

Now, Grace's faith in her relationship with Gary had begun to waver. If he *was* seeing Kristy on the side, she didn't want to know. She didn't want to be forced into making a decision that could end up with ugly results yet again. She didn't want to leave her new house, but she also didn't want *another* man choosing someone else over her. If she pretended like she didn't know, then maybe, *just maybe*, it wouldn't exist.

Would that be so wrong?

"Nothing. Might as well be dead."

"Huh?" Grace jolted back to life.

"The line. The police. No answer," Gary said as he handed the phone back to his wife. "I don't see how that's possible, but I couldn't raise anybody regardless of what number I tried."

"Yeah...yeah, that *is* odd."

She tossed her phone back into her purse and swallowed hard. Her stomach growled and rumbled for attention.

"Do we have a Plan D?" she asked.

"I guess we're going to have to figure one out, huh?"

CHAPTER 10

Gary and Grace sat on opposite benches, staring off in different directions. Outside, the snow picked up just enough to look beautiful. Had they been home, gazing out of their living room window, they would most certainly have agreed about how they loved winter in central Illinois. They might have even gone for a drive around the neighborhood, seeing who had put up their Christmas decorations early. It was that kind of snowfall.

Instead, the large puffy flakes made both of them keenly aware of the fact that the train station did not have working heat. Not only that, but with no sunlight to peek in through the few tiny windows at the top of the wall, the chill in the air felt more biting than ever. The emergency lights in the corners of the lobby area consisted of a couple measly blue-tinted bulbs; not enough to provide ample light, let alone a feeling of safety. The irony of having only emergency lights on was not lost on Gary, who considered their current predicament an emergency of sorts.

"I'm hungry," Grace said.

"Well, that makes two of us."

"I thought we'd be eating on the plane. That's why I ate such a light lunch. I never realized that we wouldn't be on it."

Gary shot her a look.

"I hope you're not blaming me, because I'm in the exact same spot as you are; hungry, tired, cold, and wishing that I was flying back to Bloomington this very minute."

"Don't you mean wishing *we* were heading back?"

"Yeah. . . *we*. That's what I meant to say."

A few beats passed before Grace spoke again.

"You said you were in a bakery earlier. Was there anything to eat in there?"

The mention of the bakery sent a chill up Gary's back. It was so close to the clothier and those faces -- those *deathlike* faces of the mannequins hovering inches away from his own. He shuddered and eyed Grace, hoping that she didn't detect the hitch.

"Uh, I can't say that I remember seeing any food lying around. I was looking for exits and phones, you know. I might have missed something."

Once again, as the words left his mouth, he was already kicking himself. *She's going to ask me to go back there. She's going to want me to look for food.*

"Maybe we can go back there. You know, just to look around. There's got to be something to eat. A pretzel or some old cookies. At this point, I really wouldn't care. I'm just starving."

Gary pursed his lips together and snorted through his nose. *I knew it. I knew she'd pull this shit.*

"Come on, Grace. We don't have time to go wandering around in the dark. We gotta figure out how to get out of here

– that's our priority. I'm about ready to bust the windows out. That might actually be our next move."

"I understand, but can't we do all that on a full stomach?"

"There's nothing there, okay? All those shops were empty. This whole damn train station is empty. How the hell we got tricked into this place is beyond me."

Grace switched her phone's flashlight on and shone it in Gary's eyes. He squinted and turned away.

"What the hell? Turn that off, would ya?"

"Nobody *tricked* us. You said that this was our station before we even left the hotel. I was just following *you*."

Gary got up and started to pace back and forth in front of his bench. He didn't have a good comeback. There was a ring of truth to her statement, but he would be damned if he'd admit to being wrong, especially after being called out by Grace.

"Arguing isn't going to help our situation," he said, slowing his steps. "Anyway, before we go breaking anything, I've got another idea."

"Plan D?"

"Yes, Plan D. I'll call Mike and Sarah."

"Mike and Sarah? What can they do all the way from Bloomington?"

"Well, they could get a hold of the police. They'd probably have better luck from where they're at. We're obviously in some weird dead zone."

Grace agreed.

"Yeah, that actually sounds like a pretty good idea."

Gary reached in to his pocket to pull his phone out, but stopped short.

"Damn it. I need your phone again."

"Here," she said, handing the pink rectangle over to her husband.

◆ ◆ ◆

"Hello, Mike? *Mike?* Can you hear me? It's Gary."

Gary tapped the volume lever up as high as it would go, but still couldn't get a clear enough connection.

"Mike, are you there? Hello? Mike?"

He pressed the # key, the *0,* and the speaker button.

"Can you hear me? Hello, anyone there?"

"What's wrong? Aren't you getting through?" Grace asked.

He turned the phone off for a moment before starting it up again.

"No, not exactly. I thought I heard him for a second, but it could have been static. Let me try again."

Gary dialed the number and moved around the lobby, holding his arm carrying the phone in all manner of contorted positions in an effort to find a working signal. After a number of failed attempts, he cussed at the screen and finger-punched random buttons. He stopped himself just before hurling it against the wall.

"Fuck it. Must be this building – the cement or metal or whatever the hell this piece of shit is made out of. It's blocking the signal."

"Try texting him. Maybe that would work."

A thin smile replaced Gary's sneer. He tilted his head and blinked at Grace.

"Huh. Well, it's worth a shot. I don't know if it'll carry through these walls, but what the hell. Ladies and gentlemen, we have a Plan E, all thanks to Grace Wolf."

Grace smiled and sat up, happily taking in the compliment. Gary didn't often praise her ideas, but when he did, she relished the opportunity to bask in its glow.

Gary's thumbs raced over the letters under the little screen:

Mike. Grace and I stranded in Rain.Wrong train station. Long story. Please contact police.Thx. Gary.

"Okay. Help should be on the way any time now."

"How will we know if he got the message?" Grace asked, taking her phone back.

"I suppose he'll probably text us back."

"What do we do until then?"

Gary shrugged and stretched out on the bench facing her. He draped an arm over his face and closed his eyes.

"Wait for Prince Charming to show up, I guess."

Grace frowned, crossed her arms and sunk back into the corner of her own bench. Her eyes remained wide open, almost *unable* to close out of fear, uncertainty and a gnawing desperation that was growing by the minute.

"I'm still hungry," she muttered. Her quiet words drifted off into the ether of the surrounding gloom, not quite loud enough to reach Gary's ears.

CHAPTER 11

It was close to 2:00pm when Mike's cell phone started to buzz. It continued to vibrate, stopping millimeters away from falling off the kitchen table. The White Barn bag with the candle for Gary and Grace sat nearby. A small pile of pocket change, Mike's brown Coach wallet, a black comb and a good luck coin rested on the other end of the table. Sarah's purse was in the living room, strap draped over a La-Z-Boy recliner.

Mike had gone in their bedroom to take a nap, leaving Sarah to enjoy a few hours of quiet downtime. There was something odd about his behavior; she noticed it ever since lunch at Olive Garden. Perhaps after he had some rest, he would feel more comfortable talking to her about whatever was bothering him. At least *this* time, Gary was thousands of miles away and she was *right here*. She was getting tired of playing second fiddle to that man.

After filling the hot tub and turning on the bubble jets, she lighted a few small candles and placed them around the spacious bathroom before dimming the lights. She placed a mauve-colored bath towel on top of the sink and hung her pink terry cloth robe on the back of the door.

The robe had been a gift from Mike for their eighth anniversary. Now, almost five years later, the first real signs of wear were starting to appear; loose threads, a couple seams beginning to pull apart. But she didn't want to replace it – not just yet.

That was the year that they had gone to Maine to celebrate their anniversary. Mike had planned the entire trip; seven days in Bar Harbor, just outside of Acadia National Park.

She remembered how he had really pulled out all the stops for this one. He reserved a beautiful oceanfront suite at The Harbor Side Hotel in downtown Bar Harbor. The list of amenities had taken up an entire printed page, including things like a Jacuzzi, gas fireplace, dining area, and a full size refrigerator and freezer. Not that they were planning on doing much cooking, if any, but if they wanted somewhere to keep leftovers, they had more than enough space to accommodate unfinished meals.

If lounging around the spacious suite or gazing at the ocean from the private deck off of the master bedroom wasn't on the agenda for their day, they had a wide list of other conveniences from which to choose. The spa packages featured such luxuries as facials, massages, nails; anything that needed rubbing or rejuvenating was at their disposal. All they had to do was pick up the phone.

Mike had also booked a whale and lobster tour prior to their arrival. He had wanted to surprise Sarah, knowing how much she loved whale watching from one of their earlier vacations to Hawaii. After boarding the boat and being welcomed by the captain, the lead officer laid out the course for the whale sightings. Sarah had squealed and practically jumped out of her seat once she realized what kind of tour it was, much to the other tourists' enjoyment. They laughed and shared in her excitement. Mike didn't mind at all. He loved the fact that Sarah was so happy. He was also grateful that he was able to provide her with such an opportunity.

When the tour had finished, the passengers were systematically funneled through a hallway and an exit door that led right into the gift shop. If any sea creature could be embroidered onto something, this place had it covered. Towels, hats, beach blankets, tee-shirts, shorts, bathrobes and more were there for the choosing. Half of the shop was geared toward children; everything set at eye level and priced three times higher than stores on the main strip in Bar Harbor.

"Pick out anything you want," Mike offered, placing his hands around his wife's waist.

"Oh, Mike. Look at the prices. They're ridiculous."

He smiled and kissed her.

"Don't give it a second thought. As far as I'm concerned, this is still part of the tour. Why don't you take a look around and if you find something, I'll get it for you, okay? Deal?"

After browsing through piles of tee-shirts and dish towels and pictures of sea birds, Sarah eyed a bathrobe on a rack near the line of cashiers. It was big and fluffy and pink, but the best part was the tiny whale emblem embroidered on the front left lapel. She thought it was adorable. From its blowhole, a little shower of drops spouted upwards toward the collar.

"Oh, Mike. Look at this."

"That's pretty cute. Ooh, and soft, too. Do you like it?"

She nodded and smiled.

"Try it on. Make sure it fits."

"Okay," she said.

She slipped it off the hanger and slid her arms through the holes.

"Oh, my gosh. This feels wonderful." She hugged the robe around herself and tied the belt.

"Well, how do I look?"

"Like we're going to need another suitcase."

They laughed as he helped her out of the robe.

"Anything else that catches your eye, hon?"

"No," Sarah giggled. "The robe is more than enough."

Mike looked at the price tag. His mouth fell open at the same time his eyebrows raised.

"Whoa. Looks like I better sell another house or two," he joked, giving her a wink.

She playfully shoved his shoulder and smacked him on the butt as they moved into one of the seemingly endless lines that were forming in front of the row of cashiers.

◆ ◆ ◆

Sarah had almost drifted off to sleep herself; the pink bathrobe being the last thing she saw before closing her eyes and laying back against the wall of the tub. The jets of the water bubbled with a white noise that comforted her and lulled her toward a pleasant repose. The four plum-scented candles took turns winking in the darkened room, helping to create the perfect atmosphere for easing a busy mind.

Just as the vision of being back in Bar Harbor was taking over, a voice pierced the solitude with a blood-curdling scream.

Sarah's body jolted up and out of the hot tub like a rocket. Water splashed everywhere; soaking the rug, dousing the candles, covering the walls. The force of the sudden displacement of water even caused the ceiling to take a hit.

On the way out of the bathroom, she grabbed her robe to cover herself. Mike's screams continued but she couldn't make out what he was yelling. The only thing she knew was that raw terror was emanating from their bedroom.

"Mike," Sarah screamed, running into their room at full force. "*Mike!*"

Mike was on the bed, thrashing about, arms in the air, legs kicking at phantom attackers. He was sweaty and pale and shouting at the top of his lungs. She raced to his side and put her hands against his shoulders, yelling into his tormented face.

"*Mike! Wake up! Can you hear me?*"

Sarah's hundred and thirty pounds against Mike's hundred and eighty-seven were virtually no match for one another. In the chaos of the moment, he smacked his wife right across the nose with an out of control flailing arm. In the next second, a single stream of blood coursed from her left nostril, passed her lips, down her chin and dotted the bed linens.

"*Mike! Stop it!*" she yelped, putting her hands to her face and moving away from the bed. Her hands caught the warm, red liquid that poured from her face. In the moment, she grabbed the nearest thing off of the dresser to hold against her nose – Mike's light blue tee-shirt.

Mike gasped for a breath and bolted upright. His eyes and mouth popped open, but his screams fell silent. In those first few seconds, he was disoriented. The world felt disjointed and surreal and he wasn't certain that the nightmare was really over.

"Mike?" Sarah said, still pressing his tee-shirt against her battered nose. "Mike, what's happened?"

He blinked hard and put his hands over his eyes.

Cautiously, Sarah approached the bed and sat next to him. Holding the shirt to her face with one hand, she placed her other hand on his leg.

"That was crazy. You were having one hell of a dream."

He rubbed his face and took a deep breath. Life was starting to settle in again – his house, his bedroom, his wife. Nothing bad was happening here. Nothing he had to fight against.

"S-Sarah?"

"I'm right here, hon." She rubbed his leg and scooted closer in.

"I…I had the worst dream…," he whispered.

"Do you want to tell me about it?"

As he took in a long, stilted breath, an audible shudder wheezed out through his airway. They sat, side by side, on the sweat-soaked sheets. Perspiration continued to ooze from his pores, but it seemed to be slowing.

"What – what happened to *you*?" Mike said, pointing to her nose. "Oh, God, did *I* do that? I don't remember anything but the dream."

"Don't worry. You just clipped me when I tried to wake you up. The bleeding'll stop in a few minutes."

"Oh, God, Sarah," he said, trying to stand.

"Mike, please. Sit down. You're still shaking."

"Is it broken? Oh, Jesus, I can't believe I hit my own wife."

"You didn't hit me. You were rolling around screaming. It was my fault, really. I was trying to hold you down. I got in too close."

Mike put his head in his hands and mumbled something about spousal abuse. With her free hand, she caressed his back and told him everything was going to be alright.

"Look. I'll go get cleaned up, get some ice for my nose, and then you can tell me about this dream. You'll feel better once it's out in the open. At least, that's what I've always heard."

Mike nodded. "Okay. But, seriously, what about you? We can have a doctor look at that. I'll get my coat on right now and we can go."

Sarah shook her head.

"No, I'm fine. Honestly. Just give me a few minutes. And, uh, maybe change *your* clothes? You're pretty drenched."

He looked down and touched his chest. His white tee-shirt clung to his body like a second skin.

"Wow. Yeah, you're right. I'll wash up, too, I guess."

"I'll use the guest bathroom," Sarah offered.

He nodded again. Still feeling a bit shaky, he rose from the bed and tested his footing. The carpet felt good underneath his bare feet – something solid and sure. He took a step toward the master bath, using the nightstand for support. She watched as he made his way toward the door.

"I'll check on you in a few," he said.

"Sounds good, slugger," Sarah joked.

Mike didn't respond. He didn't find anything particularly funny at the moment.

◆ ◆ ◆

Fifteen minutes later, Mike and Sarah were sitting at the kitchen table; a pot of hot water and two cups with teabags rested in front of them. Mike preferred Darjeeling, but Sarah had always been a fan of Oolong. Steam rose from their individual mugs, twirling into the air and disappearing seconds later.

Sarah had a bandage across the bridge of her nose with balls of cotton tightly pressed under the left nostril. It wasn't pretty, but it worked in a pinch. She wore her pink bathrobe over a pair of shorts and a Nike tee-shirt. Mike was dressed in grey sweatpants and a green tee-shirt, all of which were clean and dry.

"How's the nose?"

"Still there," she answered, somewhat nasally. "You'll have to aim better next time if you want me to stay down for the count."

Mike frowned and glared at his wife.

"Sarah, it's not funny. I could've really hurt you."

"But you didn't. And I know you certainly didn't *mean* to do anything like that."

"No, of course not."

"It was an accident, plain and simple. Now, come on, tell me about this dream."

Mike inhaled slowly and picked up his cup. He sipped carefully, trying not to burn his lips on the hot liquid.

"Alright. It's pretty bad, though. You sure you want to hear this?"

"Hey," Sarah said, pointing to the bandage on her face. "I think I earned that right, don't you?"

He cracked the smallest grin and put his cup down on the table.

"Okay, but don't say I didn't warn you."

"Consider me warned. Now, *tell* me already. I'm growing old from all the waiting."

Mike cleared his throat and spoke.

"You know how it's difficult to tell where a dream starts, right? Well, the first thing I *remember* is that the four of us were riding on a train in Germany. By four, I mean us an' Gary and Grace. That part was actually pretty nice, you know? Traveling through the countryside, passing snow-covered mountains and small Bavarian towns. Really picturesque -- something you might see in a movie."

"Sounds great so far. Except for having Grace as a travel companion. But go on, sorry to interrupt."

"Well, it doesn't take long for things to turn ugly, and believe me, it has nothing to do with Grace being there. So, we're all on this train, having a good time looking at the scenery, when Gary says something about being on the wrong train. We think that's a weird thing for him to say so we get our tickets and schedules out. You know, to check and see if he's right or not."

"Was he?" Sarah asked.

"Yeah. Yeah, he was. Right around the same time we're realizing that we got on the wrong train, this conductor comes into *our* car. He starts at the far end so we can't really see him, but we're watching him collect tickets from all the other passengers in front of us. You know how they do, take the ticket and punch a hole in it or something."

"Yeah, go on."

"So, as he's coming toward our group, I say to Gary that we should just tell this guy about the mix-up and ask him to help us get on the right train, you know? Gary agrees, so we're all just kind of talking and waiting for the guy to get to the back where we're sitting. Finally, he's close enough to where we can see his uniform, his cap...everything except his face 'cause he's looking down as he's punching tickets. That's when Gary says something in German."

"Gary doesn't know German," Sarah said.

"Well, in the dream, he does. So, he says something, I don't know what. Probably about being on the wrong train and asks what to do now. And that's when the conductor lifts his head."

Mike shuddered and took a large swig of tea. It burned going down. He ignored the pain and continued.

"The guy…the conductor, didn't have a face. I mean, it was more like a skull with pieces of dead skin hanging off. One eye was hanging and the other one was gone. His hands…God, his hands were just bones. He said that we were on the right train. The right train and the right track. *Track Nine*. That's when everybody else in the train car – you know, the other passengers, all turned around and looked at us. They were all dead, Sarah. They were all rotting corpses."

Sarah stared at Mike, clinging to every word, mouth agape, eyes wide.

"So, of course, I start freaking out. I turned to look at Gary but now he's a corpse, too. And when I looked at you guys, to you and Grace - it was the same - decaying bodies with grinning skulls. I'm screaming and screaming, but all I can hear is the conductor saying *Track Nine, Track Nine, Track Nine* over and over again, like that Beatle's song. You know the one where John keeps saying 'number nine, number nine'"?

Sarah nodded; mouth still open.

"I'm still yelling and trying to stand, wanting to get out of there. But as I get up, all of you guys start ripping into me – my clothes, my hair, my skin. I think that's probably when I hit you.

I was trying to fight everybody off of me. I guess that was when I woke up."

Sarah snapped her mouth shut, finally realizing that it had been hanging open during most of Mike's entire story. She took a drink of her tea, now tepid, and set the mug down. She eyed her husband and took a deep breath.

"Jesus, Mike. That *was* a hell of a dream."

CHAPTER 12

"Has Mike answered your text yet?" Grace asked, her voice echoing off the station walls.

"Hngh?"

"Mike? Did you get a response? You texted him over two hours ago."

Gary yawned and stretched. He had actually managed to snag a little shut-eye before being awakened by his wife's petulant questions. He swung his legs off the bench and planted them on the floor before rubbing his hands over his face.

"Why'd you wake me up? I was sleeping."

"Well, I wasn't. I was waiting for his answer."

Gary stood, allowing the blood to return to the lower half of his body. He massaged his legs and then cupped his hands together, breathing into them for warmth. It felt like the temperature plummeted while he had been asleep. If he had to hazard a guess, he would have pegged it at about 45 degrees, if that. He dug his gloves out of his coat pocket.

"We might have to break out some more clothes from the suitcases if it gets any colder in here."

"What about Mike?"

"He's probably warm enough."

"Very funny, Gary. I was talking about the text message."

"I gave you your phone back. Don't you remember?"

Although Gary couldn't see her expression very clearly, Grace's face went red. She completely forgot that he had used her phone because his screen had been shattered. Without a word, she reached into her purse and checked for any updates.

"Nothing."

"What?" Gary asked. He placed a leg on the top of a bench and stretched forward.

"No answer."

"Well, maybe he's getting lucky. I know I wouldn't answer the phone if *I* was," Gary chuckled.

An image of Kristy flashed through Grace's mind and she literally bit her tongue to stop her nagging worries. *Not right now*, she thought. It wasn't the time and it certainly wasn't the place.

"What are we going to do, Gary? It's getting late. I'm hungry an' cold an' tired an' I don't want to stay here overnight. Can't we go back to the hotel somehow? Can't you try and break the door down? You said something about breaking the glass."

"Yeah, I did. But I'm not stupid. That glass had to be inches thick. If I did manage to put my foot through it, I'd probably cut my leg to shards. I don't want to take that chance. Especially not at night. Maybe in the morning when it's light and I can see better. No, I'm afraid we're stuck here until tomorrow at this point. But if you can think of something else that we *haven't* tried, I'm willing to discuss it."

They sat in silence over the next few minutes, both contemplating their situation. Grace clicked her phone on.

"It's 9:07."

"That doesn't change anything. And it's not a helpful suggestion."

"I know. I just wanted to tell you what time it was."

"You know, if this hadn't happened, we'd be in the airport right about now, waiting to board. I'd probably buy one of those little beer steins, you know, from those kiosks that we saw on the way in."

"Yeah. They were pretty cute as far as beer steins go."

"I was hoping to pick up a few of them for some of the guys at the office."

"Yeah. I bet they would have liked that."

More silence hung between them. Lost in thoughts, plans, and potential rescue scenarios, each sat facing different directions, gazing into the bleak nothingness as time crawled forward. Gary's decision regarding *this* train station as opposed to the *right* one had begun to haunt him now. He had been so certain, *so sure*. Now, there was a hairline fracture running through his confidence and he was at a loss of how to repair the damage.

"Hey, how many bars does your phone have?" Gary asked.

"Two."

"Good. Try to keep from using it, okay? We might need that power if we manage get a signal."

Gary cleared his throat again, but with more vigor this time.

"Are you okay? You're not getting sick, are you?" Grace asked.

"No," he answered, clearing it again. "I think it's the cold. It's not doing my sinuses much good, I can tell you that."

She made an *mmm* noise, clicked off her phone and put it back in her purse. Stretching her legs out on the bench, she tucked her carry-on behind her head like a makeshift pillow and laid back. With her hands jammed deep within the pockets of her coat, Grace closed her eyes and yawned.

"My turn for some sleep," she mumbled.

"Shit. That's it."

"What?" Grace opened an eye.

"I can't believe I didn't think of it before. How stupid of me. That's it, though. It's perfect."

Grace sat up and turned to face her husband. H actually sounded rather upbeat.

"What are you talking about? What's *it*?"

"The train. Why didn't we think of that? We're in a damn train station and neither of us thought about just walking right through the tunnel. Shit, we're as good as out of here."

"What do you mean? Aren't the train cars blocking the way?"

"No, not completely," he said, as he sat next to her. "The train goes through the tunnel, right?"

"Yeah, sure. Even I know that."

"But the train isn't so wide that it takes up the entire area. That's how engineers and maintenance people get around. You know, to fix signals or work on the tracks. And that is exactly how we are going to walk right out of here. Once we're free, we can figure out what to do next. Hell, that'll be the least of our worries. We might even be able to get another flight to-night, but at least we won't be locked up in here anymore."

"You want me to walk through that tunnel in the dark? Carrying my luggage? On train tracks?"

"Look, it's not like the tracks are functioning. There's no danger of another train coming along."

"I don't know. It still sounds dangerous."

Gary ran his hands through his hair. For a brief moment, he entertained the idea of just going without her. The very thought of it was enticing but he knew he really wouldn't act on it. Somehow though, he would need to convince her to follow him into the tunnel. It was going to be a matter of logistics, plain and simple. If they were careful and took their time, they would be out the other end before they knew it.

"I tell you what," Gary started. "Why don't you wait here with our stuff and I'll go scout it out first. If I can get through to the outside, I'll come back and we'll go together. How's that sound?"

Gary could almost hear the wheels turning in Grace's head. She was as far away from having an adventuresome spirit as humanly possible, but he knew that she wanted to leave just as much, if not more, than he did. That fact alone might be all the motivation she would need to get on board with his plan.

"Think about it, Grace. If I can get through that," he point-ed toward the tunnel, "then, I'd say we're about thirty minutes to an hour away from freedom. Doesn't that sound good?"

It did. It *did* sound good. How could she say no?

"Okay. Yes. I'll do it. As long as you go first to make sure it's safe. That'll be Plan...where were we, F? G?"

"I don't remember, but whatever letter it is, it'll be the last one we're going to need. Give me your phone. I'll need the flashlight."

"But I'm scared. I don't want to sit here in the dark all by myself."

"Here, take mine. It'll work well enough for what you want."

Once they exchanged phones, Gary piled all of the suitcases on the bench next to Grace.

"Okay. Stay here and I'll be back as soon as I can. I'm not sure how long a train tunnel is, but if it leads to the outside, who cares, right? Give me at least an hour. It's what, 9:30 now? If I'm not back here by 11, call me."

"But you said the phones don't work. How can I call you?"

He sputtered. "Look, I-I don't know. Just give me some time to get to the other end. Okay?"

"I guess."

"Hey, you want to get out of here, don't you?"

"Of course. Do you even have to ask?"

"Well then, this is the way. I could still kick myself in the ass for not thinking of this earlier."

"At least you thought of it."

"Yeah, that's true. Better late than never, I guess. As soon as we're out, I'll get a hold of Mike and tell him what's going on. I'll probably never hear the end of this one."

"Gary? Please be careful."

"I will."

“It’s so dark down there…,”

“I know,” Gary said. He turned toward the tunnel and walked forward with the phone’s light in front of him, illuminating every step.

CHAPTER 13

With one hand running alongside the train cars and the other hand holding the phone, Gary cautiously made his way, step by step, toward the mouth of the tunnel. From what he could see, the second car was half in and half out. As he neared the opening, he held the phone higher in order to get a better sense of how large the area actually was.

The masonry of brick, cement, and steel looked peculiar. He was by no means an architect or engineer, but he had sold enough houses and dealt with enough inspectors to know a shoddy piece of work when he saw one. The over arching structure looked to have been a rushed job. The bricks were unevenly laid and the metal rod support beams were bent, rusted through, or nonexistent. He was beginning to wonder if the structure would even hold up long enough for him to escape through the other end.

As Gary took his first step into the archway, still using the body of the train car as a reference point, he shone the light up and around. There was a gap of at least three feet between the top of the train and the ceiling of the tunnel, but not much more. However, the space between the side of the car and the side wall was more of a concern. He was not a large man and he could ditch the winter coat if he needed to, but the first step into the maw was already making him claustrophobic.

He turned sideways and pressed himself against the smooth surface of the train, inching his way along. The periodic tug on the back of his jacket made him cringe. There wasn't much room to maneuver, to adjust positions. It was tight, dark and dangerous.

"Come on, Gary, you can do this," he whispered to himself. "Fuck the coat, just go."

He didn't like being out of his element and this was already far beyond that point. He wished he had taken off his coat before starting, to hell with the cold, but he was too far in. As he eased through, his shoes kept getting caught in between the wooden sleepers. He found the whole process to be a conundrum. He couldn't keep the light on the tracks *and* see into the tunnel at the same time. What if he ended up twisting an ankle or breaking a toe? *Then what the hell would he do? Call for Grace to rescue him?*

Once he managed to edge his way past the second car, he felt a sense of relief. The worst of it was over. Now all he had to do was walk down the set of train tracks until he reached the end of the tunnel. His right arm, fully extended with the phone's light guiding the way, gave him a small boost of confidence.

"Back to the proverbial cake walk," he smirked. "I'll be out of here in no time now."

He took five full steps before falling head first into a large hole. The tracks he had followed had come to an abrupt end right in the middle of the worm's anus.

◆ ◆ ◆

Grace bolted up and off the bench as soon as she heard her husband's screams. Her feet couldn't move fast enough as she trotted toward the tunnel, Gary's cracked phone dimly lighting her way.

"Gary? Gary! What happened? Where are you?"

"Grace!" he screamed. "Don't come in here! There's a hole!"

She stopped at the mouth of the tunnel, bracing herself against the behemoth of the passenger car.

"I can't see you. *Where are you?*"

"I fell. I'm hurt. Where are *you* right now?"

"I'm standing at the opening of the tunnel. How bad are you hurt? What happened?"

Gary lay on his back at the bottom of a ten foot dirt hole. Amazingly, Grace's phone was still intact and had landed face up and lit, about six feet away on a clump of dirty rags.

"Can you come any closer? It's hard to keep yelling like this," Gary shouted, hands cupped around his mouth, projecting his voice as far as possible.

"I'll try," Grace shouted back.

Gary wasn't sure if Grace would be up to such a challenge. If she took her coat off, held her breath, sucked in her gut, and ignored the scraping bricks along her back, she just might be able to slip through. That would be on a good day, and today was most certainly *not* a good day.

Grace would get winded from having to climb the stairs at the Redbird Arena, where Gary and some of the other agents would go to watch the Illinois State University basketball team play. The spouses would almost always tag along for the free games and the free food that was offered in the specialty boxes. On the rare occasions that Gary was able to talk Grace into going, she'd complain and gripe until he reminded her about the buffet. But the steps always remained a daunting challenge to her. If Grace couldn't handle a few flights of stairs in a clean well-lighted arena, how would she manage *this* hurdle?

While he waited, Gary took stock of the physical injuries he had sustained from the fall. As much as he could surmise, he stepped into a large hole where the railroad tracks should have been. He guessed he fell about ten or twelve feet straight down, landed on his back *(was that a good thing?)* on what felt like solid earth, and was able to move his legs. He couldn't see how wide the pit was, but from listening to the echo of his own voice, he figured it was rather large.

"Grace? How are you doing? Can you manage up there?"

He didn't hear anything, so he called out again.

"Hey! Grace? Are you able to get past the train?"

Grace popped out from the door of the second train car and perched on the edge of the cavernous hole. She shone the light from the phone down into the pit. It wasn't very bright, but it was better than nothing.

"Oh, my gosh, Gary. How in the world did you end up down there?"

He adjusted his position, trying to see up and over the wall of the hole. The light, as dim as it was, shone a little too bright for his eyes. He put a hand up to block to beam.

"Grace, will ya move the light? It's right in my face."

She did as he asked.

"How did you manage to get past the train so quickly?"

"I didn't go on the outside. The door on the first car was open and I just walked all the way through."

Surprised by her ingenuity, he couldn't help but praise her.

"That...that was good thinking. I should've done that." He hated the fact that she outsmarted him, but had to give her credit just the same.

"Are you really okay? That was no easy fall," Grace said, waving the light back and forth on her husband's face.

"I-I think so. Got the wind knocked out of me, but I think I can walk."

"What about the hole?"

"Hang on a second. Let me get your phone first. It landed on a big pile of rags down here. Talk about lucky. We've still got one working screen."

"Yes, I see it. It's over there," she said, pointing to the pile.

Gary shifted his body and tucked his legs up. With some awkward effort, he managed to push himself to his feet and rise into a standing position. His body was not happy with the change. His legs, arms, and torso felt like one big bruise and the first hint of a monster-sized headache was starting to rear its ugly head. His brain ached and throbbed angrily with every step. He lumbered over to the pile to pick up the phone.

"It still works," he said with a note of glee. "Give me a second to look around. Maybe there's a ladder or something I can use to get back up there." He cringed. Every syllable he uttered sent shots of pain through his skull.

"Okay," Grace said. She kept flashing the light from his phone on and off until he told her to stop it.

"Don't waste energy," he scolded. "We don't need to use both phones at the same time."

She leaned over and pouted.

Every step he took made him feel like his body was on the verge of retaliating. Gary didn't think that anything was broken or knocked out of place, so why did he feel like he went twelve rounds with a heavy-weight boxer and lost. *Badly*. How was it possible for *hair to hurt?*

With the flashlight app once again leading the way, Gary swept the walls that surrounded him. He had guessed right; it was a ten foot drop or so from where the tracks had ended so abruptly. As he studied the bottom of the hole, he could see that bulldozers had been at work here. Patterns made by large scoop shovels were still tattooed into the earthen walls. But there were no machines or vehicles now. As a matter of fact, there wasn't much of anything, with the exception of some rag piles like the one on which the phone had landed.

He went over to the little heap that had cushioned Grace's phone and examined it. He picked one of the pieces up and held the light to it.

These weren't rags. These were pieces of clothing. And they were covered with dried blood.

"Grace?"

"What?"

"We need to get out of here."

In the dark, Grace rolled her eyes and pursed her lips together, making her face resemble a toad.

"Really, Gary? I was hoping we could stay."

"I'm not shitting around with you. There's something weird going on here."

"What? What did you find?"

Gary had a quandary on his hands. He knew if he mentioned the bloody clothes, Grace would come unhinged and he simply couldn't deal with that. He dropped the stained shirt back on the pile and scoured the rest of the hole in a slow, methodical manner.

Small piles of bloodied clothes were scattered throughout the entire pit. Some looked as if they had been soaked through while others were simply torn and ragged. As unsettling as these discoveries were, Gary stopped cold when his foot hit something that was propped up against the far wall.

He pointed the flashlight down and gasped. He glanced up, closed his eyes and sighed. From where Grace was, she couldn't possibly have seen it and for that, he was grateful. He only hoped Grace didn't *hear* his startled reaction. He stared, unblinkingly, at the horrific find.

It was a human skull, or rather, part of one.

"What, Gary? What's going on down there?"

"Nothing," he lied. "Everything's fine."

"Did you find a ladder? Anything else that you could use to climb up?"

He scanned his immediate area and saw nothing that would help him scale the dirt wall.

"No. No ladder. Just, um, some rags. A bunch of rags actually."

Grace, still feeling particularly proud of her passage *through* the train, called down toward Gary.

"Why don't you tie a bunch of those rags together and use that as a rope. I can tie one end to the railing on the train car up here."

Damn it, Gary thought. *That made pretty good sense.* Grace was most certainly on a roll.

"Uh, well, sure. Another good idea there. Your cozy mysteries are really paying off tonight, huh? Give me a few minutes to get some of these things together."

Grace clicked the phone on and off and smiled to herself. If she wanted to play with the phone, Gary wasn't going to stop her. She was the one with all the brainstorms.

It didn't take him long to locate enough pants and shirts to create a makeshift rope. He tested each knot with a couple of strong tugs, hoping it would suffice. He tied a couple of shoes on one end for some counterweight.

"Alright, Grace. You ready to catch this? I think I made it long enough. When it gets up there, just take the shoes off and tie that end to the railing. But tie it tight, okay? As tight as you possibly can."

She clicked his phone off and stuck it in her pocket.

"Okay. I'm ready. Go ahead and throw it."

Gary's body was screaming in defiance against all of the physical activity, but he couldn't allow it to stop him. He took the shoes in his right hand, stepped back like a pitcher and hurled it upward as hard as he could with an audible grunt.

Grace held out her hands like a three-year-old catching a football for the very first time. Fortunately, Gary's aim was true. She clapped her hands together straight out in front of her and somehow managed to make contact with the shoe-end of the clothesline. Gary held up the phone to provide some light.

"I got it," she squealed.

"Okay, good. Take the shoes off and...,"

"I know. You already told me," she shouted back.

Removing the shoes, she took the first pant leg and tied it to the metal railing on the back of the second train car. She took out Gary's phone, held it in her mouth with the light on, facing down toward her work. Once she finished, she yanked on it to make sure the line was secure. Then, taking the phone, she held the light up to check on the knots.

"Gary! You said these were rags!"

"Shit," he mumbled.

"These are clothes!"

"Please don't look, please don't look," he whispered.

She screamed. "*Bloody* clothes!"

"Damn, she looked."

"Gary, whose are they? What happened down there?"

"Don't worry about that now. Just help me get out of here. Make sure it doesn't come loose as I start climbing, alright? I'm going to start now."

Between sniffling, wiping tears away and repeatedly asking Gary unanswerable questions, Grace managed to steady the makeshift rope long enough for him to scale up from the depth of the pit. During his ascent, he swore he had felt another skull or two, but since the phone was off and in his pocket, he wouldn't have sworn to it. Instead, he pretended that the smooth, round surfaces that he touched on the way up were rocks.

Once at the top, Grace reached out her hand. He gripped it as if both of their lives depended on it. She helped pull him up, straining every muscle in the process. They fell together in a jumbled heap next to the train car.

"Oh...oh, man. My whole body hurts."

"Mine too," Grace added.

"Thanks for the help," Gary said.

"Didn't you see the hole when you were walking through? How could you miss something like that?"

Gary cautiously shook his head, trying to keep the migraine that was waiting for him just beyond the shadows, at bay.

He set her phone on the ground between them; the light cast a most unpleasant glow.

"No, I didn't. If I had, I sure as hell wouldn't have taken such a dive. I'm afraid the tunnel is a dead end like everything else we've tried. Even if we were to climb back down into the pit, there's no way we can scale up the other side. For one thing, there's no train to hook the end of this line to. And the pit goes from one wall to the other wall. There's no way of getting around it."

"But where did these clothes come from? What else did you find down there?"

He looked away.

"Gary, *what*? Please tell me. Who else is trapped in here with us?"

"Nobody. It was just a dirty hole."

"I *heard* you. You found something else *besides* these clothes. Why won't you tell me?"

"I don't want to scare you, alright?"

"Too late. I'm stuck in a train station with no food, no phones, and no exits. And now we find out there's this huge hole with bloody clothes in it and track that ends for no reason. I think I'm past being scared, Gary."

He looked at her across the hazy beam of light that shone between them. Her eyes brimmed with tears and her bottom lip was aquiver. He didn't want to make things worse, but for a third time that evening, she had a valid point.

"A skull. To be honest with you, I think there was more than one. I think people died here."

Grace blinked once, twice, three times. She opened her mouth to say something, but fell backwards into a dead faint instead.

CHAPTER 14

The digital clock on the kitchen stove buzzed at precisely 5pm, a timely reminder for Sarah to start heating the oven in preparation for dinner. She had planned on making her homemade lasagna and toasted garlic bread, one of Mike's favorite dishes. He was put in charge of whipping up a salad, something he rather enjoyed doing. They both enjoyed cooking, so it made the task of fixing dinner convenient; either of them could take up the fork if the other one was going to be late from work.

Mike had calmed down from his nightmare and finally assuaged his guilt from his inadvertent swipe at Sarah's nose. Now, he was in the den studying the latest weather reports for both Germany and Illinois. The desktop computer sat squarely in the middle of a mid-sized cherry table. The screen cast a warm glow over the room. The left side of the desk housed neatly stacked papers and travel magazines, leaving the right side clear for any current projects. It was here that Mike kept all of Gary's information; schedules, itinerary, and random notes about Munich.

Gary and Grace were supposed to arrive on the 11:55pm flight at Gate 3 in Bloomington. Mike and Sarah had talked about both of them going to the airport to meet them, but with her nose being compromised, he didn't think she would feel up to it anymore. Either way, he planned to leave the house by 11:15 at the latest. After a nine hour flight, he couldn't fathom keeping his friend waiting. And he imagined that Grace would be on *this side* of impossible and crabby at that point. He chuckled and shook his head, picturing Grace nagging at Gary for the duration of their flight.

"What'cha doing, honey?" Sarah called out from the kitchen.

"Checking the weather and the flight updates. I want to make sure their plane took off on time or see if there's any delay."

She peeked around the corner, an oven mitt in one hand.

"Everything look okay?"

"According to what I've seen, everything is right on schedule. It doesn't look like the weather will be much of an issue either. A few light flurries. Nothing to worry about."

"Any stopovers?"

"Yeah, one. Gary said they'd be switching planes in Detroit, but the layover should be less than an hour."

"That's not too bad. Did you check the weather there? In Detroit?"

"Just about to."

"Okay. Well, let me know what you find. I'm going to start dinner."

He went back to weather.com and was about to narrow his search for Detroit Metropolitan Airport (DTW). Instead, the screen blinked, the computer made a popping sound and the entire machine shut off. He rebooted and sat back as it went through its paces. It whirred back to life for a few seconds before the screen flashed twice and went dark again. Less than ten seconds later, a single white line of text appeared in the center of the black background:

An error has occurred and your link no longer exists.

"What the hell?"

He shut the whole contraption down again and restarted it, taking an extra moment to make certain that he wasn't fat fingering any of the keys. After the usual warm-up, the machine resuscitated itself. With its cursor blinking and waiting for its next command, Mike typed in the DTW website instead of weather.com and scrolled through pages of information.

"Let's see," he said. "Flight 5632 from Munich. Here we go."

He touched the screen, following the line of numbers with his finger to see if their layover was also running on time. As his eyes caught up the updated information, the computer clicked off again.

"Son of a...,"

"What's the matter?" Sarah shouted.

"The computer. It's shut down twice on me now."

Sarah set the grater and a large block of mozzarella cheese on the counter near the sink. She grabbed a paper towel, walked into the den, and flipped the light switch on. Mike squinted; the sudden change caught him off guard.

"Hey, warn a guy before you do that next time, will ya?"

"Sorry, hon. You want to keep 'em off?"

"No, that's alright. I gotta take a look at this thing anyway."

"What's wrong with it? It was fine this morning before we left for lunch. I was on Facebook and sent a few emails to the girls at the office. Didn't have any problems whatsoever."

"Well, there's something going on now and I'll be damned if I know what the problem is. I've never had this kind of thing happen before. Do you remember when we got this?"

"The computer? Oh, geez, I don't know…maybe a year and a half ago?"

"That's the thing," Mike said, shaking his head. "It's not that old; it shouldn't be giving us any problems. Not yet, at least."

He sat down on the floor, reached around the back of the computer and pulled on a few cords, testing for loose connections. He took the can of compressed air from the bookshelf next to the desk and sprayed around the vents and openings.

"Maybe it just needs to be cleaned. Hell, I don't know."

"Why don't you try it again," Sarah encouraged. She tossed the paper towel in the waste basket next to the desk. "I'm going back to my cheese."

"Trade ya," he said.

"Not on a bet, mister."

She turned and disappeared around the corner. Mike let out a deep breath and put the computer back underneath the desk. He pulled his chair up to the desk in front of the screen, hit the *on* button and waited. Just as before, a gentle mechanical whirring and familiar beeping resonated through the den, lulling its owner into a false sense of security. He typed and hit *enter*.

The screen blinked on, off, then on again before freezing on the following message:

An error has occurred. Gary Wolf is dead.

CHAPTER 15

Grace's eyelids fluttered open. Gary was sitting beside her, holding her right hand and rubbing her shoulder. The phone was lying next to her head, light beam on and shining up toward the ceiling of the tunnel.

"Grace? Grace, how are you doing?"

She put a hand to her face and rubbed an eye. For the briefest of moments, she had forgotten where they were, but a throbbing, angry bump on the back of her head shoved her back into reality. It was still dark, she was still hungry, and they were still trapped.

"Gary?"

"Right here. You passed out."

"What...what happened?"

"I told you about the hole and what I found and then you fainted. We're still in the tunnel, but I'm out of the hole, obviously. Besides for that, nothing much has changed. You've only been out for a few minutes. But, damn, it sure sounded like you smacked your head pretty hard."

She sat up with Gary's help and reached around to feel the growing goose egg through her hair. A pulsating *thud, thud, thud* had already come knocking. She wondered what she was going to feel like in a few hours if she felt this bad *now*. A sickening feeling ran through her gut. She wanted to find a bathroom. It hurt to think, to move her eyes, and to turn her head.

"I wish we had some ice," she moaned. "And some aspirin. Can we look for a bathroom? Or maybe some food?"

Images of the bakery and the clothier popped up in Gary's mind. He wiped it away. No, he wasn't going back there. A return visit wouldn't be up for discussion.

"Uh...yeah. I wish so, too. We could probably hunt down a bathroom, I suppose. Probably a good idea, actually."

He placed a hand on the side of the train to steady himself as he stood, offering the other hand to his wife. She took it and struggled to her feet.

"Can you make it back to the bench? We'll go through the train cars, okay? It'll be easy, just like the way you found me. Then you can lay down 'til we figure out our next move."

"Plan H?"

"Whatever."

Together, they waddled and shuffled, holding each other for support as they made the trek through the passenger car until they cleared the tunnel. Gary practically collapsed onto one of the benches; Grace did the same thing on the one facing him. They closed their eyes, drowning in their own injuries and pains. For a few moments, Gary relished in the silence, but it wasn't long before Grace's voice cut a deep swath in his meditative calmness.

"It's a little after eleven."

With his eyes still shut, Gary put his hands over his face and then let them drop soundly against the bench.

"Thanks for the update, Grace. Not sure what do you want me to do about it, though."

"It's late. I don't want to stay in here overnight."

In the dark, Grace could hear Gary sighing. She couldn't see his expression, but she could sense his frustration.

"I don't want to be in here, either. As a matter of fact, we should be on a plane right this minute, flying over the ocean on our way back to Bloomington, but instead, we're stuck in some godforsaken defunct train station in the middle of nowhere."

"It's not *nowhere*. We're in Rain."

"You know what I meant, Grace. You really want to have this discussion *now?*"

Gary opened his eyes, looked skyward, and then decided he liked things better when they were closed. It created a sense of distance from the awful reality of the situation. If he couldn't see it, there was a remote chance that it wasn't happening. *Wasn't that how it worked in those horror movies that he and Mike loved to watch?*

He also didn't want to argue semantics with his wife or explain their circumstances ad nausea. All he wanted to do is go to sleep until help arrived – probably sometime in the morning. To hell with finding a bathroom at this point. They could take turns squatting in a corner for all he cared.

"Gary?"

He exhaled again, adding a groan at the end for emphasis.

"What. Grace."

"I can't feel my suitcase. Or my carry on."

"What do you mean you can't feel it?"

She pulled her phone out, clicked on the light and scanned the benches.

"They're gone."

"What's gone?"

"Our bags. The luggage. Look, they're gone."

Reluctantly, Gary opened his eyes and followed the light's movement. It was just like watching some amateurish shaky-cam found footage film. He followed the beam's path as she highlighted each bench, the floor below them, and the area around the train. The bags were gone; she was right about that.

"Holy shit, Grace. What'd you do with them?"

"What do you mean *'what did I do with them'*? I was in the tunnel with you."

"You were supposed to keep an eye on them while I was trying to find a way out of here."

"Well, I wasn't going to drag them into the tunnel with me. I heard you yelling and I ran over to try and help."

"You were the last one to see them, Grace. Where the hell did they go?"

He hoisted his aching body off the bench and pulled his phone from his pocket. He searched the area again, just in case she missed something, but they had disappeared. Just another fact to add to the mounting tally of unfortunate circumstances.

"They were *right here* when I heard you yell from the hole. You sounded hurt, so I got there as fast as I could. I was only trying to *help* you."

With an effort that caused more discomfort than it should have, Gary began to pace back and forth as his hands took turns running through his hair. The longer he stewed, the harder it became to contain his anger. The internal heated froth had bottlenecked over the past few hours and finally hit its boiling point.

Rage swelled from inside his gut and bubbled out of control. His face reddened and contorted; beads of sweat appeared along his hairline. He gritted his teeth. His breaths came quick and shallow. He was seething; a reaction that Grace had never witnessed before. He stopped pacing, grabbed her by the shoulders and forced her to stand. From that point, he let the throttle open all the way.

"Grace, *you stupid bitch*! You have been nothing but a pain in my ass ever since we left the hotel. All you do is whine and moan over and over again. *'I'm tired', 'I'm hungry', 'when are we gonna eat?'* Well, I've got news for you. We are stuck in this shithole until tomorrow morning when I assume someone with a key will find our carcasses fast asleep. So, for the love of God, stop whining and stop telling me what time it is. *It doesn't matter*. We've missed our flight. There is no other train. We are stuck. That's it. End of story."

His voice echoed off the walls until all that was left was a disquieting ring that ping-ponged around the lobby. He turned away from her and headed toward the engine. A twinge in his lower back sent his body into one large spasm, giving him the appearance of a zombie walk-on character in a movie rather than a disgruntled husband.

Grace stood motionless. Her lower lip trembled and the sting of tears welled up in her eyes. It wasn't *her* fault. *She didn't lose the suitcases. She was trying to be helpful.* She reached up to brush a hair strand away from her face, not knowing how long she could refrain from the emotional downpour that was seconds away. She sniffed and blinked and cleared her throat, but it was too late.

Grace started to bawl.

"Jesus," Gary muttered. He had made his way over to the front of the engine, out of sight but not out of earshot. A few more steps and he could almost make a run for the corridor; perhaps hide in one of those little shops until help arrived. If only he wasn't so dedicated to the sanctity of marriage. To his loving wife. *To her bank account.*

He took a deep breath and went back to the bench. She had a death grip on her purse and as he got closer, he could see that she was fishing around for some tissue.

"Grace?" He stepped closer, illuminating the way with his broken phone.

"Go away!" she sobbed, blowing her nose into a crinkled Kleenex.

"Grace," he lowered his voice. "Look. I'm sorry. I-I shouldn't have said those things. I was mad and I took it out on you and I shouldn't have. I know exactly how you feel. I'm tired and hungry, too. And after that fall, I gotta tell you, I think it shook a couple of nuts and bolts loose."

She giggled and put her hand on his leg. It made him cringe.

"Do you forgive me?"

She wiped her face and turned toward him. In the phone's glow, she looked puffy and red like an angry blowfish.

"Of course I do."

She reached over for a hug and he let himself be embraced by her cold and sweaty body. He was first to break from their clammy seal.

"Good, alright then. How about we start over and get serious about some things? Now that we don't have any of our stuff, it might put a real kink in us getting out of the country. Do you have your passport?"

She rummaged through her purse and pulled out a small blue folder.

"Yeah, right here."

"Good. I have mine in my jacket. That'll be one less hurdle to deal with tomorrow. Was there anything in the suitcases that you can think of that could be critical?"

She thought for a minute and shook her head.

"No, I don't think so."

"Good. As long as we've got money and our passports, we should be okay. Awkward, but manageable."

"But what *happened* to our stuff? Where'd it go? I thought we were alone in here."

Her question slapped him in the face. As much as he tried, he couldn't fight the image of those bloodied mannequins. But this time, instead of imagining them falling backwards with those ghastly faces staring up at the ceiling, he pictured them shuffling down the body of the worm, their stolen suitcases gripped in their ruddy-colored hands – the very same hands that had held clumps of human hair. What if they *were* back? What if, at this very minute, they were watching as Grace had her melt down while he tried to make amends?

◆ ◆ ◆

Gary Wolf was not normally a fearful man. The oldest of Diane and Spencer's three children, he was born and raised on the outskirts of Bloomington, Illinois. Gary and his brothers grew up not wanting for much. Sports and school had always come easy to him. Friends were plentiful as was his parents' attention. He was showered with gifts on all the routine holidays as well as his birthday, and he was *so* well liked, not even his two siblings were jealous of him.

The only worry that Gary could never seem to shake was a fear of store mannequins. He didn't recall having firsthand knowledge of what happened on that particular Saturday in October over thirty-six years ago, but thanks to his mom, he had heard the story enough to be able to repeat it, almost verbatim.

As she told it: She and Gary, who couldn't have been much older than three, had gone into Bergner's in Eastland Mall. They were shopping for one of his dad's birthday gifts, a blue Izod shirt to go with a sweater that his mom had picked up earlier in the week. As they stepped onto the escalator, Gary's tiny hand firmly gripped three of his mom's fingers. They chatted away about presents and cake and things that a three-year-old might find fun to talk about.

Once they reached the top of the escalator, Diane Wolf helped her son off the step and whisked him around to the left, heading toward the Men's Department. At the same moment, a stock clerk was removing one of the undressed mannequins from a display platform. The collision between the two was enough to jar the mannequin loose from the clerk's grip. The body fell with a distinct and hollow thud, but the force caused the head to fall off. The disembodied head rolled directly toward Gary's feet, stopping an inch away from his blue tennis shoes. The mannequin's painted face stared blankly, lips barely parted in a skewed smile.

Gary screamed and covered his face with his hands, too petrified to run or to move. Dianne picked him up and tried to comfort him, but he would have none of it. He cried and fussed until his mom agreed to leave the store. The next day, she returned to Bergner's, leaving Gary at home with a babysitter for the afternoon.

◆ ◆ ◆

Grace repeated her question about who could have possibly taken their things and Gary did his best to ignore it. Instead, he suggested that she forget about everything else and concentrate on going to sleep in order to pass the time.

"Maybe I'll just try my phone again," Grace said, more to herself than to Gary.

"No. I don't want you wasting any power. Your phone is the only thing that's really working right now. How many bars do you have left?"

"Still two."

"Well, save 'em. Who knows…we might be able to make some calls tomorrow morning."

"Can I play with your phone then?"

"Grace," Gary sighed. "Why can't you just go to sleep?"

"I'm not that kind of tired. My head hurts too much."

"Fine. Here," he said. "There's only one bar left. And from what we've experienced so far, I don't think you'll be able to do much with it."

He settled back down on the bench opposite his wife and closed his eyes.

"Wake me up when we get rescued."

"I'll be sure to do that," Grace said, kicking back on her own bench. The shattered glow from Gary's phone cast a deathly pall over her face, giving her an odd sense of comfort.

CHAPTER 16

1 December, 16:55

Pieter Hinter, Zoning Supervisor and lead on the demolition project, stepped into one of the office conference rooms carrying a large clipboard under his arm. The six other men who were already seated at the rectangular table collectively turned their heads toward the door with a jeweler's precision. Papers shuffled and throats cleared. There was a general consensus to rise when the large man entered the room, but he held his hand out to dissuade any such motion.

"We don't have time for such formalities. We have too much to review before tomorrow morning."

A murmur spread among the men. Folders were open and pens clicked. The group was poised as a unit, ready to hang on every word.

"We have assigned a man who will make a final sweep inside the station later tonight. I don't expect anything unusual to be discovered, but we are taking all the precautions that we can. Mr. Heinrich and his associates will be setting up the perimeters on the outside. No one without permission will be allowed near the building after the grounds have been secured. That is scheduled for 0700. Mr. Gerig, what is the latest status from your unit?"

"We have secured the surrounding areas up to a three mile radius. Homes, businesses – everyone has been alerted."

"Good. Most of the equipment is already onsite. The emergency departments, police and fire, will meet with us at 0800. The initial blast is set to detonate at 0900."

"Sir?"

"Yes? Question?"

"Yes, sir. I am curious...what is being done about the train in the station?"

"Train? There is no train housed in the station."

The questioning man looked at the faces of the others around the table.

"No? But there was, yes? An engine and two passenger cars. I remember seeing it for myself when we last swept the interior."

Pieter Hinter shifted in his leather seat. He reached for the glass of water in front of him and drained it before eyeing the man who asked the question. He glanced around the room, painfully aware of the silence. All eyes were on to him, waiting for an answer. Pieter cleared his throat before speaking.

"That is true. There *were* cars in the station at one time, but they have since been removed. The building is empty."

"Please, if I may ask...what happened to them?"

Pieter fidgeted with his pen and refilled his glass from the pitcher of water on the table. He downed the liquid in record time. Thin lines of sweat raced down his back. He pulled a handkerchief out of his pocket to wipe the sweat from his forehead and upper lip.

"Sir? The train?"

"It has been burned," he barely uttered.

The six men leaned forward, hands cupped around their ears, attempting to hear the breathless comment.

"Terribly sorry, Mr. Hinter. We could not hear. Could you repeat that?"

"*Burned*. The cars," he hissed, biting off each word as it left his quivering lips.

The young man raised a hand, still unsure of how to proceed.

"I-I don't understand. Why not leave the train in the station to be destroyed with the rest of the building? Everything at once – would that not be more efficient?"

Another brave soul chimed in, adding more questions and commentary.

"Yes, why not? Better yet, why burn such a quality piece of machinery? Something like that could have been dismantled and used for parts. If nothing else, that material could have been used for scrap metal."

Pieter Hinter rose from his seat and walked to the window which overlooked an empty field. The sun had disappeared and there was a palpable chill emanating from the glass. It made him shudder. Every time he exhaled, a little opaque cloud appeared in front of him, drawing his eye toward *it* instead of the outdoors. He used his sleeve to wipe it away. Finally, he turned back to face the group of curious men. When he resumed, it was all he could do to speak just above a whisper.

"The bodies. They…they wouldn't come off. My men tried. They scrubbed and labored for days, but still they remained. Blood stains, pieces of skin, remnants of organs…no matter how hard they worked or what tools they used; the dead would not leave. It was as if they had merged to the last place they were alive. No one could not pry them off the seats. The windows. The floors. After a while, the workers came to me. They asked not to make them return to the train or to the station. They offered to do anything else. Clean toilets, scour the streets. Anything but work where there was so much death."

The group of men sat motionless and listened. They nodded their heads and ingested every word of the story. After a lengthy and awkward pause, the young man who asked the first question raised his hand again.

"Sir, if I may?"

Pieter acknowledged him with a slight nod.

"I-I don't mean to be morbid, but weren't all of the bodies exhumed from the station when the accident first happened?"

"We recovered everything that we could, Mr. Meingalt. But even a man who has worked in a morgue or an emergency room has limits."

"Are you saying that there could still be bodies that *haven't* been recovered?"

"My reports state that there are no bodies in that building and I will stand behind that conclusion. As far as all the districts involved are concerned, the only remains left in that station are the ghosts who haunt it. And that, Mr. Meingalt, is why it must be destroyed."

CHAPTER 17

Gary was on the verge of sleep, oblivious to the beeps and blips his phone was making as Grace continued to press buttons. He had been correct; she couldn't get the internet which meant no Facebook, no games, and no searches of any kind. She was, however, able to get into his email.

Even through the cracked screen, she was able to navigate his list of contacts, scrolling down the list of names, recognizing some and dismissing others as clients or co-workers she had never met. After a few more swipes, a list of text messages popped up.

Grace looked toward Gary, now sound asleep on the bench opposite her. Her eyes had become accustomed to the dim lights in the lobby, well enough to recognize her husband's slumbering physique. However, it was certainly *not* bright enough to tell if his eyes were really closed...or barely open and spying on her.

She fidgeted on the seat, waited a moment for a reaction, and then rustled her coat. When Gary didn't stir, she sighed and leaned back against the bench, focusing on the phone's screen. Through the shattered pieces, she read:

> ***1814 Werner Way: Interested in…***
> ***Will my lawyer be able to…***
> ***About 109 Turning Leaf…***
> ***When are u cuming home, lover?***

Grace sat straight up, feet flat on the floor, mind already reeling. She re-read the last line again and felt her own face go flush. She eyed Gary; *was he truly sleeping or just pretending? Was this a set-up? A test to see if she trusted him?* She cleared her throat and coughed in order to get a response – her *own* test, to make absolutely sure that he hadn't orchestrated this text himself, as a ploy to catch her snooping.

No. He hadn't moved or made a sound. Whatever she was about to see was no ruse. She touched on the entry and began reading.

> *Hey Lover G. Been waiting a week now. Can't wait to see u Tues night. Hope u brought me something from Germany, 'cause I've got something for u. Give u a hint – it's hot 'n steamy and needs your hole attention. c u soon. Kris.*

Grace dropped the cell phone into her lap. She didn't even try to fight back the tears. Streams lined her cold face, dripping down and onto her lap, making the smallest *puck, puck, puck* sound against the nylon material of her jacket. Her gut chimed in, growling in anger and disgust and dismay. But it wasn't from hunger this time.

A lump formed in her throat next; a hard little nub that could have gagged and choked the very life out of her. After a few dry, forced swallows, it dissipated into a reasonable nodule. Despite the near freezing temperature in the station, she started to perspire.

Sweat rivulets were born and traveled south underneath her thick layers of clothing. If she had been home, in a more comfortable setting, she would have locked herself in the bathroom and allowed the waterworks to flow more freely. She would sit on the little rug in front of the sink, cry for at least an hour, and replay everything that she might have done wrong during the past six months, because somehow, *she* was the one to blame.

Then, and *only* then, would she have allowed herself to clean up, get it together, and make dinner before Gary got home, pretending that everything was fine. If he would have asked why her face was puffy and red and looked like she had been crying, she would say that a darn Lifetime movie must have hit a little too close to home. She couldn't tolerate a confrontation. It was out of the question.

Gary moaned and shifted. He mumbled something inaudible.

"Hey," he said a bit louder. "Did you hear me? I asked you what time it is."

Grace didn't reply. She continued crying into a crumpled tissue.

Gary moved around, trying to find a position that was a little less painful. His lower back danced in and out of spasms and the hard wood of the bench wasn't helping matters. He could barely make out the round lumpy silhouette of his wife, but he could certainly hear her sniffling and fussing, loud and clear.

"*Jesus, now what?*" he muttered, shifting to a sitting position to mirror hers.

"Grace, what could possibly have happened from the time I closed my eyes to now to make you start blubbering? You've been sitting in the dark and I've been asleep. What the hell?"

Stopping in mid-sniff, she picked up his phone from her tear-stained lap and hurled it at him. It glanced off his temple and skidded across the floor behind him.

"Why don't you ask *Kristy* what's wrong?"

Rubbing his head where the phone clipped him, Gary shook his head and sputtered a reply.

"Wha-? Why'd you throw the fuckin' phone at me? You hit me in the head, you know that? Shit. What'd ya go and do a thing like that for?'"

"It's almost one in the morning. You can ask Kristy anything else, 'cause I'm done talking to you."

"Grace, would you please tell me what the fuck is going on and why you're talking about my office assistant who happens to be 3,000 miles away? Great...I think I'm bleeding."

"She's not *that* far, according to your messages. As close as the next text, obviously."

He fingered the cut on his head, trying to determine how serious the scrape was. One thing he *was* sure of; the next question out of his mouth would not be met with the slightest shred of empathy.

"Grace, could you take a look at my head with your phone? I think it's cut pretty badly, but I can't tell."

"You've got to be kidding. You want *me* to help *you*?"

"*You're* the one who threw that thing at my head. It's the least you could do. And while you're up, you should find my phone from back there, wherever it landed. You're the only one with a working light now."

Grace said nothing. She was having her own internal battle as to what her next move should be. While it was true that she threw his phone and injured him in the process, technically, it was *his* fault. It was *his* message from *his* office assistant that prompted the whole drama.

She always had the feeling that Gary had been carrying on with women throughout their relationship, but she never had undeniable proof before. Now that she did, in her own hands no less, she was stymied as to what to do with the information. If she ignored it, pretended that she misread the message, it would basically allow him to continue the charade, yet enjoy *her* money and *her* home in the process. If she confronted him, neither of their lives would be the same. Her mind zigzagged back and forth, trying to decide on how best to respond. After being married for only two years, it shouldn't come to this. It was their belated honeymoon after all.

"Grace, give me your phone. If you don't want to help me, fine, but I still need to use the flashlight."

She reached into her pocket and gave it to him.

"Here."

"Thanks," he said, touching his head and shining the light on his hand. A thin streak of blood was visible on two fingers -- nothing dire. He gave the phone back to her.

"You need to fire Kristy when we get home."

He held his coat sleeve against the cut, putting as much pressure on it as he could despite the awkward angle.

"What?"

"When you get back to work this week, I want you to fire her. Not suspend her or give her a few days off...*fire* her."

He scoffed. "I'm not firing her, Grace. You're not going to tell me how to run my business and you're certainly not going to tell me who I can hire *or* fire. I'm through with this conversation. Now, could you go get my phone?You remember, the one you *threw* at me and probably broke beyond repair?"

"Fire her or I'm leaving you."

Gary turned to face his wife. Even though seven feet of space separated them, he could have sworn he felt her staccato breaths against his cheek. Her voice was on the verge of cracking, yet there was an underlying strength to it this time. It was also clear that she was seconds away from more tears.

"Listen to me. Pay close attention, Grace. I am not firing Kristy or anyone else for that matter. And you are not going to leave me or threaten to leave me anymore. In the morning, we will get on a plane and fly back to Bloomington and will go on with our lives. After you've eaten and had some decent sleep, you'll realize that you've been overreacting to this whole situation and that a cooler head prevailed - *mine*. And if you won't get my phone now, that's fine. We'll get it in the morning. Lie back on your bench, close your eyes and just rest if you can't sleep. And for God's sake, stop crying."

Grace stood, took a step toward Gary and hesitated. She spun on her heels and started toward the engine.

"Where do you think you're going? What are you doing?" Gary called out.

"I'm not sleeping near you. I'll sleep on the train."

Gary stretched his legs out, covered his cut with the other coat sleeve and shut his eyes.

"Wonderful."

CHAPTER 18

After reading the computer's cryptic message about his best friend being dead, Mike threw up his hands and said the whole thing was bullshit. He called Comcast and argued with each person up the chain of command. No one was able to restore his faith in technology, let alone their exaggerated claims of the company's good customer service. For over forty-five minutes, Mike fought with two services representatives, one supervisor, and a lead retention specialist. It was almost six o' clock by the time his brain hit overload with all of the unrelenting circular conversations.

"We can send a technician out to your house, sir," the supervisor offered. "Just understand that if it's a problem with *your* computer, you'll be charged for it. The service call is fifty-five dollars regardless of what they find."

"My computer and my connections are not the problem. There's something screwy on *your* end," he said.

"Everything looks fine on our end, Mr. Waverley. We aren't seeing anything out of the ordinary. It's probably a loose cable somewhere. Things like this happen when the weather gets bad."

He was done with the pointless banter, so he eventually agreed to let a technician come to the house and *check for loose wiring*. It would probably end up being a waste of time and money, but at this point, it was more about the principle of the thing. *Somebody* needed to do *something*.

"Fine. Tomorrow at four then," he said. Scheduling the appointment didn't make him feel any better, but he didn't know what else he could do.

Mike sat in front of the dark screen, arms folded across his body, his eyes closed, deep in thought. There was a sense of things being *off*, but he couldn't quite put his finger what that thing might be.

The hallucination at Olive Garden. The head in the back seat. The horrible nightmare. Now, the computer. Mike didn't necessarily consider himself to be a religious man, but he couldn't deny the feeling of trepidation that hovered over him. Was somebody trying to tell him something? Or were all of these just a bunch of random, weird happenstances?

He would feel better if he could talk to Gary. It was a long shot; with the time difference, Gary and Grace were probably somewhere over the ocean right now, but there was nothing to lose in the attempt. He picked up the phone and dialed. After letting it ring, it clicked over to voicemail, so he left a message.

> *"Gary, this is Mike. When you get a chance, could you shoot me a text or call me. Just checking in to see if everything is good with you guys. Thanks."*

He set the phone on the desk and crossed his arms again. He could try Grace's phone too, but he didn't have a sense of desperation yet. She would automatically assume that he was checking up on the two of them and that could only lead to a *nagfest* for Gary. He refused to put his friend in that situation, unless he had no choice.

Mike popped into the kitchen where Sarah was fussing over a bowl of uncooked brownie batter. He grabbed a teaspoon out of the drawer and scooped up some chocolaty goodness.

"Mike!" Sarah yelped. "That's for dessert."

"No," he said, pointing to the greased pan in front of her, "*that's* for dessert. This is just a little pick-me-up."

Exasperated, Sarah positioned her body between Mike, his spoon, and the bowl of batter. "Go away. I'm trying to finish dinner."

"Oh, don't worry," he joked, tossing the licked-clean utensil into the sink. "There's plenty left for dessert."

She smirked and continued stirring.

"Hey, I'm thinking of calling the airport. You know, just to be sure."

She stopped in mid-pour and looked at Mike. "Oh?"

"Yeah. I'd feel better if I knew everything was still on schedule."

"You couldn't get any answers from Comcast? I heard you talking to them in there."

He rubbed the back of his neck. It felt stiff. His shoulder and back muscles were on the verge of a mutiny as well.

"Ah, they were no help. Big surprise there, huh? By the way, they're coming over tomorrow to make sure our wires aren't crossed."

"Huh? What do you mean?"

"Never mind," he said, gesturing as if to erase the comment from mid-air. "I plan on being home when they come. I just wanted to let you know. When do you think dinner'll be ready?"

"I'd say around six-thirty, maybe closer to seven. Do you really have to call the airport? Don't you think that's a little...I don't know...excessive?"

Mike shook his head. "No. Well, maybe. It would make me feel better."

"Well, let me know if you find anything out."

He went back to the den, sat down and faced the dead computer screen. He thought about turning it on again, maybe booting it back up and taking another run at it, but he didn't.

He was afraid of what he might see.

◆ ◆ ◆

"Blue Airways, ticket counter. This is Brittany. How many I help you?"

"Hi, yes, uh, I'm calling to check on a flight that's supposed to be arriving at 11:55pm tonight. Can you tell me if flight number 5632 from Munich is on time? I think they have a stop-over in Detroit."

"One moment, please, while I check for you."

Mike heard the dulcet tones of insipid Muzak along with the occasional spoken advertisement for *convenient airline travel as close as your keyboard*. He doodled Gary's name on a piece of scratch paper as he waited for Brittany to return.

"Sir? Yes, that flight is scheduled to arrive here at Gate 3. Is there anything else I can do for you?"

"Um, yeah. Could you tell me if two passengers are on it? Gary and Grace Wolf?"

"I'm sorry. We're not allowed to give out that information."

"Please? It's rather important."

"I'm sorry. We are unable to give out any information regarding any of our passengers."

"Okay...I understand. Thanks."

"Thank you for calling Blue Airways. Have a wonderful night."

Mike tossed the phone on the desk and leaned back in his chair with a heavy sigh. Of course they wouldn't tell him anything. Just like *he* wouldn't give out any information about any of his real estate clients.

"Shit," he muttered. "Sarah?"

"Yes?"

She trotted into the den, wiping her hands with a paper towel.

"I think I'm gonna take a quick run over to the airport."

"Really? What'd they say? Is something wrong?"

"They wouldn't tell me anything. Not on the phone anyhow. I might be able to get a little further if I could talk to them in person. I won't be long."

"Oh, Mike. Do you really think that's necessary? I mean, this is all a lot of commotion just because our computer is on the fritz. To be honest, I really think you're making too much out of all of this."

"It's just something I have to do. I can't explain it any better than that."

CHAPTER 19

Armed with her only belonging, Grace held her purse against her body and climbed up the steps of the second train car, the farthest one possible from Gary. She wanted, no, *needed* to put as much physical distance between the two of them as she could safely manage. With everything that had happened over the past few hours, the last thing she wanted to deal with was the fact that her husband was having an affair. If the *possibility* of it was bad, having seen the evidence to *prove* it made it all the worse.

Her mind spun. She was mentally exhausted and her body was numb. As she walked down the center aisle heading for a seat in the back, she brushed against the hand railings. The lightest contact sent a ripple of shockwaves through her being. It was as if every nerve had lost its protective sheath and had been laid bare for all to see.

Once she reached the very back, she took a seat and placed her purse against her leg. Methodically, she tracked the phone's light around the area to get a better look at her new surroundings.

Pairs of blue plastic-covered cushions lined each side of the aisle; the outermost seats were fortunate to have a window view. Thin posts of steel ran down from the ceiling and into the base of the floor—bars for passengers to grip during their travels. Oblong rows of light fixtures ran along the top of the car; now they were dark and still. The grey mosaic patterned floor looked as if it had been licked clean. She couldn't detect a single mark, a bunny of dust, or a wayward paper wad.

The size and the configuration of the seats would have made it difficult if not impossible for anyone over the age of four to stretch out and sleep in them, but Grace was weary enough to try. She scooted her back against the window and stretched her legs out in front of her. It wasn't often that she was grateful to be of short stature, but this was one of those special occasions. She wiggled her butt into position; her feet dangled off the seat and into the aisle.

With the purse now resting in her lap, she placed her hands on top of it and checked her phone. *Two bars. Don't waste them.* She turned it off and sat in the dark, allowing her mind to take her wherever it wanted to go.

Gary.

Was he planning on leaving her for Kristy when they got back to Bloomington? Would she have to face yet another divorce? Sure, she had money, but she didn't want to be alone. The first breakup, the one with Ed, was bad enough; a second time would likely destroy her. How could she possibly go on without him, if that *was* his intention? What if he had been using her just to get to Europe? And why did people continue to use her and then throw her away like a piece of garbage after they had their fill?

◆ ◆ ◆

Ursula Stanton was a year older than Grace when she was assigned the desk next to her in 1974, at the start of sixth grade. Ursula had been held back a year because the administration determined that she had difficulties respecting authority figures and spending one extra year in elementary school would fix the problem.

Grace had been ecstatic about entering her final year in the grade school building. It would be the last time she would be grouped in with the little kids. Once this year was over, she could say that she was in *junior high*, and at thirteen years old, a statement like that meant something.

Before the first week was through, Grace and Ursula were already comparing notes about boys and teachers and everything else that was important in the life of a sixth grader. Over the next few months, they became inseparable. In and out of each other's homes, they shared the same posters and issues of *Tiger Beat* and *16* magazines. They knew every word to every song on their favorite records. They played them so often that Ursula's dad threatened to break the needle on the stereo *if he heard that side played one more time.*

Grace spent many weekends at Ursula's house for sleepovers. They loved watching late night television and raiding the fridge after Ursula's parents had gone to bed. When the girls tired themselves out enough, they would finally crawl under the covers of Ursula's queen size bed and giggle over the latest school gossip.

Grace couldn't have been happier. Being fairly shy and overweight in grade school didn't make life very easy, and making friends had always been a bit of a challenge. Having Ursula as her best friend was like a miracle after years of putting up with loneliness and bullying. She would have done anything for this girl and assumed Ursula felt the exact same way. Grace was positive that the feeling was reciprocal because right after Ursula turned fourteen, she taught Grace about *the special game*.

This *special game* was something that Ursula introduced Grace to during one of their sleepovers. She explained that since she was a woman now, having had experienced her period for the first time, there were secret physical needs that had to be met. And if Grace was *really* her best friend, she should be willing to help in any way that she could.

"Of course," Grace agreed, "I'll do anything you want me to do."

Completely content with manipulating her lackey, Ursula showed Grace exactly what to do and how to do it. She would take off her pajamas and lay on her back with her left arm out to the side. This was Grace's signal to lie down next to her friend. Then Ursula taught her how and where to kiss her body. She also showed her how and where to rub her genitalia.

At first, Grace was hesitant. She didn't understand why these things felt good and why Ursula never did anything to *her*. But her friend had quick and dubious answers at the ready. Ursula explained that Grace was supposed to pretend that she was a boy; one of the members of the band they liked so much.

Ultimately, Grace did as she was told. She convinced herself that she should be happy to have such a mature and knowledgeable friend, even though there was something unseemly about the whole experience. As naïve as Grace was, she often wondered about this secretive game. Something about it felt *wrong*, but such things were not discussed or talked about during those years.

The roles were never reversed. That option wasn't ever discussed, not that Grace really wanted to. Even after she turned twelve, it would be another three years until *her* first period. The idea that Ursula might be gay had never crossed Grace's mind until much later. And if Ursula *was* gay, did that make *her* gay in the process?

In February of 1975, Jacqui Frei, a new girl, moved in with her family right next door to Ursula. She was in eighth grade and came from the *big city* of Chicago. Grace never saw it coming.

One Friday night in early March, Grace had walked the two blocks to Ursula's house with a small overnight bag in her hand. Mrs. Stanton let her in and told her to go on upstairs; the girls were already up there playing.

The girls?

Grace stepped through the bedroom door, just as she had done dozens of times before, but tonight was different. As soon as she cleared the threshold, Ursula grabbed Grace's bag and tossed it under her desk while Jacqui shoved Grace into the double-wide closet. Jacqui picked up a jump rope from the floor and weaved the thick cord around both of the handles, trapping her in. No matter how hard Grace pushed on the doors, they wouldn't budge far enough apart for her to escape. The more she kicked and pounded and threatened to tell Ursula's parents, the more the two older girls ignored her.

During a quieter moment when Grace was trying to catch her breath, Ursula warned her that unless she shut up, they would leave her in there for the whole night. Grace yelled for Ursula's mom and dad, but the other girls laughed and said that they had already left for the evening. *You can yell and scream all you want but no one will ever hear you.*

Hours later, the two older girls turned out the lights and crawled into bed for the night. Grace had completely worn herself out from fighting, crying, pleading, and struggling. She was hungry and needed to pee. But *mostly*, she was terrified. She could hear moans and giggles in the dark and wondered how long they planned to keep her locked up. *What if she suffocated? What if she died? What if Ursula stopped being her friend?*

In the morning when she woke up, Grace readied herself to do battle with the closet doors, but they opened without a fight. According to Mrs. Stanton, the two other girls had already left.

"They were down here early, ate breakfast, and left for the park. If you hurry, you could probably catch up with them, dear."

She sipped her coffee and didn't bother to look up from reading the paper.

That was the last time Grace slept over at the Stanton household. That was also the last time her best friend spoke to her. From then on, Ursula spent every possible moment with Jacqui; both of them pretending that Grace never existed.

◆ ◆ ◆

Grace took out her last semi-clean, semi-wrinkly tissue from her purse and wiped her eyes. As the memories of sixth grade began to fade into shapeless clouds, a strange vibration swept through the train car. Instinctively, she held her phone and purse against her body. She wondered if Gary had sensed the same sensation.

The tremor felt like a low-grade earthquake, something that Grace lived through once before, back in the late 80s in Normal. It hadn't been a *bad* experience. Nothing had fallen off the shelves and she didn't remember anyone being hurt, but it was still a strange thing to have happed while living in the mid-west.

This was different. It was as if the car itself took in a long, deep breath and then shuddered as it exhaled. Grace sat deathly still, waiting to see if it would happen again. As the minutes passed, she allowed herself to relax. She loosened the grip on her purse and settled back against the window. Her eyes closed and she felt herself drifting off to sleep.

In the next moment, a cutting chill careened through the inside of the train. Ice instantaneously covered every surface, shattering the bulbs above the seats. *Pop! Pop! Pop!* The tiny explosions rang out, one after another, startling Grace, making her jump.

When the final blast erupted directly over her head, Grace leapt out of her seat and lurched for the exit, crunching over broken glass while simultaneously bumping and thumping against the plastic seats like a sad game of pinball. When she reached the doors, her body was a clammy mass of quivering flesh. She felt hands being placed on her shoulders as others wrapped themselves around her waist. Still others pulled on her arms. These unseen appendages led her back to her seat, guiding her with unmistakable certainty.

She put up no resistance as these invisible entities enveloped her body, entering through her nose, ears, mouth, and pores. A bone-chilling burst of aggravated energy coursed through her veins at the same time her core temperature plummeted. While these ghostly spirits embraced and intermingled with Grace's soul, there was something *comforting* about their presence. Something reassuring and steadfast.

Something unholy.

And she welcomed every one.

CHAPTER 20

Mike drove to the airport in his jade green Prius, normally a seven-minute jaunt when the roads were clear and weather wasn't a deterrent. The snow was falling at a steady pace, but it was nothing out of the ordinary for a hardy Illinoisan. He made the short distance in complete silence. He didn't bother to turn the radio on or toss a CD into the player; extra distractions were not needed.

It was about 6:15 by the time he pulled into the parking lot and entered the building. Like magic, the sliding glass doors opened wide and offered entrance to the terminal. He spotted the Blue Airways counter and headed over, glad to see there wasn't a line.

A young man in his early 20s, wearing the requisite blue pants, blue vest, blue tie and starched white shirt stood at attention behind the laminate counter. A few feet away, the Delta check-in line was eight passengers deep with two customer service reps handling one question after another. Down at the other end, the American Airline staff was fielding their own hoard of commuters. Mike wondered if Gary had gotten a raw deal by going with this airline. Maybe Blue Airways was at fault all along.

"Yes, sir. Can I help you?" the young man squeaked. His name tag almost sparkled when caught by the overhead lights.

"Hi, uh...Jeffrey," Mike said, eyeing the tag. "I have a few questions that you might be able to help me with."

"Of course, sir. I'll do my best."

Mike smiled. Jeffrey was trying far too hard.

"Well, I'm supposed to pick up a friend here in a few hours, but I was having some trouble at home with my computer. I couldn't tell if the flight was on time or if he and his wife are even on the plane. I was hoping you could confirm some of these things for me."

"Well, sir, I can't give out any personal information, but I can see if your friends are listed on the manifest for the return flight. What's the name?"

"Gary Wolf. And his wife Grace. Same last name."

Jeffrey clicked away at the keyboard in front of him, stopped to read something and then continued typing. As Mike waited, he watched the line at the other counters ebb and flow. He made a mental note to ask Gary about the air fares. He had to have scored a hell of a deal to go with an unknown.

"Could...could you hold on for a minute, sir?" Jeffrey said. His pleasant demeanor had turned apprehensive.

Mike nodded. "Sure. Is there a problem?"

"Just- a, one minute please. I need to get my supervisor."

Mike let out an exasperated sigh. Were his questions really all that complicated? Even for someone as green as this kid?

Were Gary and Grace on the plane or not? Seriously, how hard could this be?

He fished his phone out of his coat pocket and texted Sarah:

> *Why do I get all the new employees? Not even sure this one's voice has changed.* ☺ *Be home soon! Love M*

He smiled, poked the send button, and tucked the phone back into his pocket.

A woman in her early 40s followed Jeffrey back to the console. She was dressed in a similar manner but she had a commanding presence. Mike noticed right away; perfect manicure, coiffed hair bun, painted on make-up, and not a loose thread to be found. She quickly scanned the man standing on the other side of the counter before turning her full attention toward the computer screen.

"Ma'am? I'm try-," Mike started.

She held up her hand to quiet him. He sighed again and shoved his hands into his coat pockets.

Jeffrey's supervisor, whose name tag read Night Shift Manager, Kelly Sparks, glared at Mike for the briefest moment. Her stoic demeanor and unemotional expression told Mike that she was already annoyed at his attempt to converse before she was ready. He looked down at his shoes and took a half step back. He didn't want to provoke any confrontation.

"If you would give me a minute, sir?"

"Sorry," he muttered, and glanced around the terminal on the off-chance that someone would have seen the brisk exchange between himself and this woman and show him some empathy. He also hoped that he didn't just lie to his wife, and that this interaction *wouldn't* take long and that he *would* be home soon.

He thought about Gary; about the day that he and Grace boarded the plane and left for Germany. They were both so excited. Even Grace had eased up on the nagging and whining. Gary had talked about this trip for a solid month; this belated honeymoon of theirs. They wanted to wait until they could agree on a destination. It had taken almost two years.

Mike never really understood why his best friend would marry someone like Grace. Both he and Sarah thought it was *obvious* that she was the wrong person for a guy like Gary. During a few get-togethers sans Grace, Mike asked him why, out of all the women he had seen over the years, would he choose someone like her. When Gary would say something about it being a good business venture, Mike never took him seriously. Maybe, in retrospect, he should have.

The one thing that Mike had noticed was the absence of the word love. Gary would use terms such as *heavy like*, or *security*, or a *solid partnership*. He would also drop phrases such as *a joining together* and *solidifying a bond*. Looking back on their conversations now, it appeared that Gary was entering into some sort of business arrangement instead of matrimony.

He wished he had paid more attention early on. He suspected that *he* loved Gary more than *she* ever could. Not in a sexual way of course, but rather with a deep-seeded alliance that would put any other relationship to shame.

Kelly Sparks, with her pristine appearance and professional attitude, finally took her eyes off of the screen and whispered something to Jeffrey. The young employee's eyes darted back and forth from Kelly to Mike at least three times before he excused himself and disappeared through an office door behind the counter. Mike approached the desk, arms crossed.

"Okay, *now* can you tell me what's going on?"

"Sir, if you would, I think it would be best if you come with me. We can talk privately in my office regarding your situation."

"No, I'm not going anywhere and I don't have a *situation* that needs to be discussed in private. I'm not sure what your policies are concerning the Patriot Act or giving out personal information, but I need to know if I should come back later or not. If they've changed planes or schedules or what the hell ever, *I* haven't been notified. Why is a simple question such an issue for everybody?"

Kelly stared at Mike for what felt like an eternity. Her blue eyes softened; her demeanor grew calm. She nervously adjusted her uniform even though there was no reason for it. It just gave her something to do with her hands.

Kelly Sparks loved being in charge. She loved the power and she loved being at the top of the food chain, even if it only meant being the night shift supervisor at a small airport in central Illinois. But during moments like these, she longed for someone else to take the lead. With every cell in her body, she wanted to tell the man standing in front of her that he would have to wait for *her* supervisor.

Instead, she took a deep breath in, held it, and let it out. Using the mouse, she clicked and highlighted two lines of text before turning the computer screen toward Mike. He looked down and followed the specified information with his finger:

Gary Wolf – Cargo Bay – Deceased.
Grace Wolf – Unspecified.

Kelly spoke in a whispered hush, clumsily placing her hand on the counter near his as a stilted gesture of comfort and concern.

"I'm sorry, sir. According to our manifest, it looks like your friend is dead."

CHAPTER 21

The ethereal *beep-beep-beep* seeped into Gary's unconsciousness. There was something ingratiating about the repetitive noise that wedged itself into the empty spaces between his dreams, and he could no longer ignore the intrusion.

His body, however, was not on the same page and did not want to cooperate. His legs, back, and arms felt as if they had been ironed and put away for the winter. Forcibly rolling onto his other side didn't do him any favors; the world as he knew it shifted. The movement sent a piercing shard of unmitigated pain and wedged it deeply between his eyes. Every twitch, every subtle change in facial expression, caused him to wince and moan and he hadn't even opened an eye yet.

He wasn't certain if it was morning or if anything had changed while he slept. Slowly opening his eyes, allowing himself a sluggish entrance into consciousness, he looked toward the bench where Grace had been. It was empty. He had a vague memory of an altercation, an argument or fight, and that's why she wasn't sleeping across from him. But no specifics were coming to mind. As a matter of fact, nothing of any real relevance was coming to Gary's mind.

With an unsteady, trembling arm, he hoisted himself up into a sitting position and placed his feet on the floor. The world spun; head over heels and back again. *This wasn't good.* A low rumble ignited in his gut -- engines roaring, gunning for the nearest way out. He fell to his knees, hands darting out to catch himself in mid-fall and threw up at the foot of the bench.

When he was able, he struggled to his feet and felt his way to another bench, doing his best to avoid the mess he made. He tried to get a bead on why he felt so horrible, but his mind refused to focus. In one moment, he was visualizing their hotel room where they had spent the past week, yet in the next, he was treated to scenes of his office back in Bloomington. Papers were scattered all over his desk as Kristy, his assistant, gathered them up. She gazed seductively at him over her shoulder as she leaned over his desk in an obviously exaggerated manner.

And what the hell was that damn beeping?

Gary couldn't quite place where he was, other than perspiring in a dark and cold room. *Was he at home? At work? A trip? Yes, he was on a trip. Was it business? Was Grace with him? Yes. She was here, too. But where was she now?*

"Grace? Grace, are you there?" he called into the emptiness, his words echoing off the walls of the dead station.

There was, of course, no answer. Grace was blissfully asleep in the second train car.

"Grace? Can you hear me? I-I don't know what's happening. I'm confused."

Gary's voice trailed off as his uncertainty grew. *Why couldn't he think straight?*

He covered his face and eyes with his hands as he swooned in and out of consciousness. More than anything, he wanted to curl back up and go to sleep, yet he fought the urge to do so. His head bobbed up and down which was not helping the nausea. And still there was the constant beep-beep-beep that droned in his ears.

He patted himself down, searching for his phone, needing to have some contact to the outside world. When he came up empty, it triggered a memory. The phone. *His* phone. That was the noise that had been driving him crazy. But where the hell was his phone?

Good. *Very good*. He was able to focus on a single train of thought. He giggled. *Train of thought.* He hadn't lost his sense of humor. If he could stay the course and figure out where the hell his cell phone was, then he could probably decipher the rest of this puzzle. For instance, *where the hell was he?* Fleeting glimpses of familiar images flashed through his brain; sites of Europe, fragments about catching a plane. He pictured Grace holding a suitcase and walking through a different terminal, but in the next second, the image was gone, replaced by a fog that clouded his reality.

The one constant, however, was the pain. Unfortunately, there was no vacillation in this regard. It was all-consuming and wrapped around him like a Black Mamba viper. His body was a throbbing pulse of discomfort, but his head was sheer agony. He was thankful for the quiet.

The beeping again. Gary remembered that he was looking for his phone. It was odd; he knew that he always carried it with him. There was a good reason for that, too. Something about it being critical for his job. Something about clients being able to get a hold of him. Wasn't he in sales of some kind? Houses. Yes. A realtor. Was he in someone's basement?

"Grace? Are you here? I can't see very well. Could you turn on a light?"

A train station. That's it. But why would he be sitting alone in the dark in the Amtrak station in Bloomington? He never traveled from there. It didn't make any sense, and yet he couldn't shake the feeling that all of this was connected to Europe somehow, and that Grace was close by.

"Hello?" He forced himself up, holding on to the back of a bench for support. "Is anyone here?"

The incessant beeping was slowing. Instead of a constant *beep-beep-beep*, it morphed and dragged into a single *beep, pause, pause, partial beep*. There was a final gasp. With its dying breath, it held a single dirge tone and went silent. Gary's cell phone was dead.

"It stopped," he said. "That noise. The beeping. It's gone."

A smile drew over his lips and for the first time since he woke, a sense of relief and calm washed over him. He stood perfectly still, appreciating the pureness of the moment. Disregarding his pain, his circumstance, his surroundings, his questions – in this morsel of time, he felt flooded with peace and tranquility. If he could only hold on to *this* feeling, he was certain that he could face any adversity to come.

Seconds later, Gary was bent over again, relieving himself from whatever was left in his stomach and intestines. This time, he didn't have the wherewithal to find a third bench with a clean area. He slumped down on the floor, missing the regurgitation by inches, and groaned himself back to sleep.

CHAPTER 22

Mike pulled the Prius door shut, threw the car into reverse and sped out of the parking lot without so much as a glance in the rear view mirror. He was trembling. He fumbled with the radio knob, inadvertently punching a wrong button which cleared all of the pre-programmed stations he had previously set. With the snow coming down harder now, he switched the windshield wipers on, and in the process, hit the *brights* as well.

"Shit."

More fussing with the dashboard only caused more frustration. He gave up trying to do much of anything else but drive home in one piece. He pulled into the garage, shut the car off, and stormed into the kitchen where Sarah was setting the table for dinner.

"Oh, perfect timing. Dinner is ready. All you have to do is sit and enjoy."

"No. Everything's far from perfect."

Sarah put the silverware down on a cloth placemat and looked at her husband. He was visibly shaken.

"Mike, you're trembling. What hap-...oh, no, were you in an accident? I noticed the snow coming down heavier."

He shook his head as he fought with the zipper on his coat. His fingers failed to cooperate.

"Dammit, I can't even get my jacket off."

Sarah helped him out of his coat. She took his things, hung them up in the closet, and returned to the kitchen.

"Come on, now. Have a seat and tell me what's going on. I don't think I've ever seen you this...this...panicky. Do you want to eat first?"

"No. No, I can't eat right now. Maybe later," he said, scooting one of the kitchen chairs out from the table. "I'm just about at my wit's end with the airport an' Gary and the computers."

"Oh, God. What happened? And, please, start from the beginning so I can get a running start with all this, okay?"

"Yeah, alright."

Mike proceeded to tell Sarah about his conversation with the airport employees. He explained how their attitude had changed once the screen had showed that Gary was dead.

"I tried to tell them that there was no possible way either of them was dead. That their computers were just as screwed up as ours and that it had to be a problem with their systems' department."

"So, what did they say to that?" Sarah asked.

"Nothing. Well, the lady said that she was sorry for my loss."

"Oh, that's nice. Did you ask to speak to the manager?"

"She *was* the manager."

"I can't believe it. What a bunch of incompetents. How in the world did someone as smart as Gary pick an airline like this one? Unbelievable."

Mike shook his head and shrugged.

"Yeah, I know. Can you imagine if *our* computer system at work had those kinds of problems? We'd all be out of a job by the end of the day."

"Really," Sarah agreed. She went back to setting the table, placing the little goose and gander salt and pepper shakers in between their plates.

"What...what are you doing?"

"Setting the table?" She half-laughed and turned toward the cabinet with the glasses. "You finished the story, right? I thought you were hungry. I know *I* am."

"No, I mean, how can you just go on like nothing's happening?"

"Uh...," she hesitated, holding a glass in one hand. "Because nothing *is* happening? You had me scared for a minute, dear. I thought you were in an accident at first. You know, the way you came in here all flustered."

Mike looked at Sarah incredulously.

"How can you think of food at a time like this?"

"A time like what? What are you talking about?"

"Gary is missing and you're standing there talking about dinner like everything's normal."

Sarah set the glass on the counter and moved back to the kitchen table.

"Mike," she started. "Everything *is* normal. Nobody's missing. You said it yourself – the computer system they're working off of is messed up. You'll go to the airport like you planned and pick them up when their plane lands. Just. Like. You. Planned. I don't think I'm going with you after all this. I'm exhausted and my nose still hurts."

"What about the manifest at the airport? It said that Gary was dead and Grace was missing."

Sarah glanced at the dinner cooling on the stove and then at the clock above it. She was on the verge of a headache from the circular conversation.

"Mike, do we really have to do this now?"

Mike frowned, slamming his cell against the table. The corner of the phone clipped a fork tine just hard enough to send the piece of cutlery to the floor, clanging like a warning bell.

"Dead, Sarah. I saw the manifest on the screen. It said he was dead. How do you expect me to ignore something like that? You know, if this was one of your girlfriends, you'd be flying off the handle, making calls, getting the police involved. You don't care because it's about *Gary* and *Grace*."

Sarah's face turned red. She grabbed the pan of brownies and chucked the whole thing into the sink. Bits of chocolate cake splattered against the backsplash and wall.

"You know, I am really getting sick and tired of this. It's always *Gary this* or *Gary that*. You're always saying 'Sorry, Sarah, I can't help you today, Gary needs me to do something'. Why is it that he always manages to come first and I end up as your sloppy second? I get the fact that you've been friends with him longer than you've known me, but *I'm* your *wife*. I've put up with a lot over the years. And yes, I've had some of the best times of my life with you, but I always felt that if it came down to Gary or me, you'd choose him every time."

Mike sat listening, mouth agape, eyes wide and unblinking as she continued her tirade. This was the first he had heard about any of this and was truly stunned. Why she picked *now* of all times to go off on him was even more baffling, and a little infuriating.

"Where in the hell is all this coming from?"

She started to tear up but blinked it away. If she was going to drive her point home, she had to hold it together while still making her case.

"I love Gary. And I don't mean *that* way. I mean as a friend, a *good* friend. I know how important he is to you. But ever since we got married, Gary's needs have always come first and mine have been a distant second. I've put up with it because I have my own life. My own job. My own friends. But this is getting old. I spent over an hour and a half making sure that you had dinner early because you asked me to. Honestly, why can't they take a cab from the airport? It's only a few miles to their house. *You're* the one that has to get up for work early tomorrow and here you are playing chauffer at midnight."

"Now, wait just a…,"

"I'm not done, Mike. So, I went to all this trouble and now because of some computer glitch, you're not even going to eat. You're probably going to get on the phone and make a lot of long distance calls to find out that nobody knows anything. You really think that a busy airport in Munich has time to track down two people? And for no real reason other than a hunch?"

"I never said that I was gonna call…,"

Sarah beat her fists on the counter; the spice rack rattled in contempt.

"But you were *going* to! I know because it's so easy to go down that rabbit hole with you! I'll bet anything that you were already thinking about calling their hotel and the airport and any other place they might have gone. Weren't you? Seriously, weren't you thinking about doing that?"

"Well, to be honest, yes…,"

"You see? I thought if you went to the airport and asked your questions, that would be enough, but then you came home all upset and got sucked right back into *Gary, Gary, Gary*. Why couldn't you just come home, have a nice, quiet, normal dinner with me and let them get a damn cab so you wouldn't have to drive out in this weather again? It's less than four miles from the airport to their house, for Christ's sakes. Can't they handle that on their own?"

The dam of tears was breaking. Sarah let out an awkward, hiccup-y sob that sounded somewhere between a cry and a honk. She turned her back to Mike so he couldn't see her face.

He got up from the table and went to her. He put his hands on her shoulders but she wiggled free of his touch. He tried again.

"Sarah, honey. I didn't know you felt this way. Why didn't you say something before?"

She shrugged, unable to speak coherently through the tears. Her body tensed as she felt the weight of his hands.

"I don't know what to say here," Mike said. "Gary's been my best friend for, geez, I don't even know how many years. I never wanted to hurt you. With any of this. You gotta believe me. I just thought you'd understand."

She spun around. Her face, ruddy and tear-streaked, contorted into a ball of anger.

"Thought I'd understand? Understand *what*? That a best friend outranks a wife? That I'll always play second fiddle because you've known him *longer*? What's the matter with you? *Let the man call a fucking cab!*"

Sarah wriggled out from Mike's embrace and ran down the hallway to their bedroom. He heard the door slam and the lock click into place.

Standing alone in the kitchen with only a dented pan of brownies in the sink and a cold tray of lasagna and bread on the stove as companions, Mike sighed. It was 7:50. His appetite had disappeared and now his wife was in tears and locked in their bedroom. He felt something nudge at his conscience; a pressing sense that he should go to her, comfort her, make everything okay again.

But what if Gary was in trouble? His best friend might need him.

Mike picked up his cell phone and started making long-distance calls.

CHAPTER 23

Grace's eyes flew open with an audible click. Her initial instinct was to remain motionless, at least long enough for her to take inventory of her own body. She wasn't in pain, other than the churning hunger that was tuned to a low rumble. Nothing was broken so she considered herself ahead of the game. *Ahead of Gary*. The last thing she remembered was falling asleep in the train. Beyond that, she was confused and disoriented because she wasn't where she should have been.

Instead, Grace found herself lying face up on the cold, hard floor of the lobby. Her purse was perched on top of her stomach, hands gripping the bag as if it was the winning ball from a World Series. As jarring as this discovery was, she was not afraid. On the contrary; Grace was the most calm she had been since first stepping foot in the station hours ago.

The slightest hint of sunrise was peeking in through the tiny windows on the perimeter; not emitting enough light to read by, but enough to help a person distinguish a human shape from a wooden bench. A quick glance at her phone alerted her to the fact that time had indeed been inching toward morning. It was 5:20am.

The station was still ice cold. How they managed to not freeze to death over the past eight hours or so, was beyond her. She sat up, legs out in front of her, and looked around. The few windows were coated in a thin case of ice. The image reminded her of old-timey mirrors in antique shops. There was something distorted and beautiful about the effect; like looking into the past and seeing yourself wrapped up in history.

Or perhaps it was more like the stained glass windows at her church. Except there were no angels or saints embedded by lead piping. And there certainly wasn't any depiction of Jesus or any of his disciples. Not even Judas. Not *here*.

There were also no cars in the belly of the worm. No engine, no tracks, no adjoining seats, no busted out overhead lights. But there *was* a tunnel, dark and foreboding, with an archway of an open maw that appeared like an endless scream. If you were reckless or careless or hopeful enough and wandered into its pitch, it would lead you down a dirt path that would end suddenly, without warning. It would drop you into a deep pit where broken body parts and desperately mangled souls had already filled the crevasses within the earth.

Grace noticed that her body was shrouded in a fine white powdery substance that reminded her of the chalk they used in grade schools. As she stood, a cloudy mist of white floated through the air around her but didn't dissipate. Instead, the minute particles were drawn back to her, clinging to her clothes and seeping back into her pores. They were a part of her now, these infinitesimal molecules, this unidentifiable matter. And that was fine with her.

She walked over to Gary, who was now sleeping on the cold ground facing away from where the train had once been. She touched his shoulder and he groaned into wakefulness.

"Gary, get up."

"Hngng...wha...," he slurred, eyes still shut to the world around him.

"Wake up. It's morning. It's time to get going."

He rolled over to face her, one eye still not cooperating. She looked like a blurry dew-drop with legs.

"Heh...wha' goin' on?"

"You said to wake you in the morning. Well, it's morning. Come on. We have a lot to do."

She clasped his hands in hers and pulled him into an upright position. His head rolled and lolled back and forth, just enough to make him sick again. His body convulsed one, two, three times, and he lost whatever remaining stomach acid he had left in his gut just to the left of where Grace stood. She watched him as he sputtered and shook. She took a step back and allowed him to go through his paces.

"You're ill," she said.

He raised a sloppy hand and wiped his face with his sleeve. He was sweating despite the frigid air in the station. Even in the dim light, she could tell that he was as pale as the white powder which covered her.

"Who you callin' ill?"

"Follow my finger with your eyes," Grace demanded. She held up her hand and moved a single digit back and forth in front of his face. He rocked his head side to side, trying to keep up, but the motion only set his stomach out to sea again.

"Urgggh...," he moaned.

"You have a concussion. Probably from the fall. That's why you're sick and not making sense."

"I dn't fall," Gary mumbled as he leaned into Grace's legs for support.

"Yes, you did. You fell into that hole in the tunnel, don't you remember?"

She stepped back, allowing Gary to slide face first onto the ground. He turned over to lie on his back and then once more to his left side, trying to find a comfortable position. As his eyes adjusted, his mouth fell open. He sputtered in disbelief.

"*Where the hell's the train?*"

He forced himself to his feet, struggling, throwing his balance this way and that. He looked back and forth between his wife and where a 300-ton train should have been. The emptiness of the lobby made him feel so claustrophobic that he crossed his arms over his body and shivered. He was under the impression that he *wasn't* dreaming, but he couldn't think clearly enough to distinguish reality from hallucination. *Was* it a concussion? Was Grace right or was all of this a compilation of being hungry and tired and injured?

"Where did the train go, Grace? I-I don't understand…,"

"I know you don't. That's why I'm going to explain it to you. I need you to follow me."

She turned and led him toward the opening of the tunnel. He shadowed her with a slow, awkward, and stumbling gait. As they edged closer, Gary craned his neck, looking around for some clue as to what happened to such a behemoth of a vehicle. How could it have disappeared without as much as a squeak to wake him?

"Did you hide the train, Grace?" he giggled and covered his mouth with a hand.

"Delirious," she whispered to no one. "He's delirious."

She stopped a few feet from the tunnel's portal; both of them standing motionless, waiting for the proper moment to continue their trek. The wide mouth was poised to welcome all who searched for the lost and the unknown. A putrid, archaic stench hissed up from the pit; an ancient greeting from those that had already passed on to the other side. Through the silence, Gary could almost hear the deafening screams of men, women and children. He could also hear the sounds of screeching metal ripping and clawing its way against the brick walls; of panes of glass and panels of iron and steel colliding against each other.

"What...what is this?" he asked. He rubbed the back of his head and tried to keep his eyes in focus.

"It's the way out, Gary. It's what we've been waiting for all night."

He looked at her in disbelief, cocking his head to one side, studying her face.

"Wha? Way out?"

She nodded.

"Yes, Gary. It *is* the way out."

"You...you mean...we can go? Just like that?"

"Just like that. You *do* want to, don't you?"

"Oh, Kristy. Yes, let's go home," he beamed.

"Why don't you go first, my dear?" Grace said. She stepped to the side to let him pass.

CHAPTER 24

Three trucks pulled up in front of an empty warehouse about a block from the defunct Rain Bahnhof at 0500. Their colorful markings conveyed a jovial atmosphere, like a circus or a traveling carnival to the casual observer. But this was not case. The orange and yellow vehicles were not there to provide mirth and entertainment. They were there for one dark purpose only: destruction.

Two men from each transport exited and headed toward a small group who had already gathered around a makeshift center of operations. Each of them was armed with a thick, black binder loaded with maps, schedules, and demolition plans. There were thermoses full of coffee on the tailgate of one of the vehicles; a few plastic bags with Styrofoam cups beside them. Some of the earlier arrivals had already downed their first cup and were well on their way to polishing off their second. The men who had driven the brightly painted trucks stopped to pick up the hot provisions before joining the ranks of the others.

A general sense of sullenness hovered over the group. As they waited for the rest of the crew to show, the conversations and snippets of dialogue were brief and halting; their words clipped and their tone, somber.

A biting chill penetrated the early morning air. The sun had just begun to show itself and it would be hours before the temperature hit double digits. The men that had gathered at this hour were well versed for these conditions and had dressed appropriately. Even so, when they weren't holding hot coffee or making notations in their binders, their hands were tucked deep within coat pockets.

Pieter Hinter, the lead supervisor of the project, had arrived before anyone else had even showered for the day. He had barely slept during the previous night. The dark circles underneath his eyes confirmed this latest bout with insomnia. There was something about this particular project that strangled his thoughts. One might think that after having worked in the Zoning Department for over seventeen years, one demolition job would be like the next. The only differences would be in the details and the locations. But this one was *different*. This one burrowed under his skin and dug a home along his marrow. The number of casualties, the feasting on the dead, the soulless eyes of the zombie-like survivors...

At least the whole damn thing was almost over.

By 0530, everyone who was expected had arrived. Plans were outlined and reviewed; questions were asked regarding specific procedures and answers were given down to the smallest minutiae. Everyone understood the gravity of the situation. Each man in attendance had labored in conditions far worse. In comparison, today's objective would be a walk in the park. This time, they wouldn't have to remove pieces of the dead.

As Pieter lead the meeting, the fire trucks and police cars pulled in behind the rest of the vehicles. Polite waves and friendly nods were exchanged. Pieter noted that the emergency crews were over two hours early. Apparently everyone was on edge this morning.

"You three will lead with the explosives once the other team has finished sweeping the external premises for the final time. They are to be affixed every few feet. Not one brick is to remain standing. Is that understood?"

Everyone nodded in agreement. Yes, this building had stood there too long. Ever since the re-construction had been put on hold, it was an ugly and garish reminder of tragedy and death. Its time was long past; it should have been destroyed months ago.

A police sergeant joined the group. He motioned at Pieter, insinuating that he wanted to speak with him privately.

"Will you excuse us for a moment?"

He and the officer stepped away from the others.

"Yes, Sergeant. What can I do for you?"

"I heard you found suitcases last night during your final sweep of the interior. Is this something we should look into?"

"Ah. The American suitcases, yes. One of my men found them in the lobby area. I was surprised to see them in such good shape. They had to have been there since the accident. I can't imagine how they were missed."

"Was there any identification?"

"No. Well, there was a partial tag in English. That's how we concluded that they were American. But there were no numbers, no airline name. Nothing that could identify the owners. One had men's clothing and the other two belonged to a woman."

The sergeant looked toward the workers who were circled around a tailgate. They were deep in discussion despite the cold and the early morning hour. These men were no doubt trustworthy and hard-working; there were no corners cut in this operation.

"How *could* we have missed them before? *We were so thorough...*," the Sergeant asked.

"They must have been found during the reconstruction attempt. Someone must have placed them there and then forgot. You remember how difficult everything became...,"

The officer looked away, avoiding eye contact with Pieter. If he had looked into the man's eyes, he might not have been able to contain his own tears. He rubbed his face and coughed.

"Yes. You must be correct. I can see you have a solid team, Mr. Hinter. I'm certain they did everything they could at the time."

"I assure you they did. As for the luggage, it has been disposed of."

"Good. *Very* good. I will let you get back then."

The men shook hands and turned to their respective vehicles. On the way to his car, the sergeant breathed a deep sigh of relief. When word about the suitcases had come across his desk only hours before, he broke out into a soul-crushing shudder. He, too, hadn't slept in days.

The sergeant knew the train station was haunted. He, along with every cop on the roster, was there that day. He saw the carnage and the torn bodies. He witnessed half-dead survivors feasting on those who didn't make it. Horrific images reeled through his mind: the faces torn in half, the broken shards of glass protruding from open wounds, the children grasping the hands of parents no longer attached to the rest of the arm. He saw people shuffling through the wreckage, tearing chunks of flesh from the dead, gorging themselves as if they were the last members of the Donner Party. It was as close to a living hell as he could possibly imagine.

Finally, the decision had been made. The crews were here; ready to demolish this ghastly building in the next few hours. Maybe this would make his own nightmares stop – the ones where headless commuters and ghoulish children would chase him through a train station that had been turned into a graveyard. Perhaps, if he were lucky, once this godforsaken place was razed, his wife would no longer have to shake him from his nighttime agonies; from the dreams that left him drenched in sweat, convulsing uncontrollably, with his mouth agape in a contorted shriek.

Perhaps now, the ghosts would allow *him* to rest in peace as well.

CHAPTER 25

Mike threw his cell phone on the coffee table, watched as it skidded across the smooth surface, only to take a nose dive off the edge and bounce onto the carpet. He curled his hands into fists and pounded them into the couch cushions. His temper was one degree away from boiling over.

"Damn. Damn. Damn!" he said, accentuating each punch with an expletive. The sofa easily yielded with each exclamation of rage.

Unable to reach anyone that knew any anything about Gary and Grace's whereabouts, he wasn't sure what his next move should be. He headed toward the computer in his den, but thought better of it. That wasn't going to help, even if he *could* get it to work. At best, it would just show information that he already knew. At worst, it would be a replay of what he saw earlier. He needed real facts and he needed them now.

One thing was certain; he had to get Sarah back on board. Whatever plan he came up with would go a lot easier if he had a partner. Enough time had passed for her to cool down and think logically about the situation. After all, Gary was her friend, too.

Mike headed down the hall to their bedroom and tried the knob. It was still locked. He knocked on the six-paneled door.

"Sarah? Sarah, come on, open up. I need to talk to you."

"I'm done talking. I'm going to bed."

"Wha-, it's only a little after nine. You never go to bed this early. Come on. I feel silly talking through a door."

There were a few beats of silence before he heard a click from her side. He turned the knob and felt it give. He sighed and stepped into the room.

"Thanks, hon. Look, I want to apologize. I didn't mean to make you so upset."

Sarah turned to look at him. Her face was slightly swollen and red; her eyes wet from tears that hadn't yet dried. She had changed into a pair of blue sweatpants and a sweatshirt instead of her usual, the pink robe. Mike was keenly aware of the wardrobe choice.

"Well, you did," she said, almost inaudibly. She sat down at the foot of the bed, crossed her legs and hunched over as if she were shooting marbles. He kicked off his shoes and joined her.

"Well, I'm sorry. I honestly had no idea that my spending time with Gary was so upsetting to you. I always thought we got along great. You wanna shot at *my* nose?" he added, laughing to lighten the mood. She ignored the offer.

"I told you, I have no problem with Gary. He's a great guy, a good friend, and a fun co-worker."

Mike shook his head and furrowed his brow.

"Then what's the problem? What am I missing here?"

"Oh, Mike," Sarah moaned. "This has nothing to do with Gary per se. It's *you*. *You're* the one that's making the choices. Gary just happens to be on the receiving end of it."

He shook his head again. Something just wasn't connecting. Mike adjusted his position to face her squarely.

"Wait. So…it's *me* you're having a problem with. It's not Gary or Grace. Is that it?"

Tears descended down her cheeks again. She didn't bother to wipe them away.

"Mike, as long as I've known you, you've *always* put Gary first."

"In what way?"

"Whenever he calls or wants you to do something, that's it. It's like nothing else matters. You drop whatever you're doing and run over there like he's on his deathbed."

"That's not true, Sarah."

"Yes, it is. I know he's your best friend. *I get that*. But you don't see me high-tailing it over to Judy's house whenever she texts me."

Mike unfolded his legs and stood. He wanted to pace around the room, but held back. He didn't want Sarah to know that he was getting agitated by her accusations.

"You're blowing this whole thing way out of proportion. I don't know what sent you into such a frenzy, but none of this makes sense. Everything's been fine 'til about an hour ago."

"I *knew* it," Sarah muttered. "I *knew* you wouldn't get it, no matter what I said or how many times I said it."

"For Christ's sake, Gary's in trouble right now. Doesn't that mean *anything* to you?"

"You don't know that. You're turning everything upside-down because some computer system is a little haywire. It's the same thing that you do all the time. It's just a different day."

"They said he's dead, Sarah. If that's not a reason for extreme behavior on my part, then I don't know what is. And if that's a problem for you, then I'm sorry, but I'm not giving up on him."

"There's nothing to give up on, Mike. You're making up a whole story in your head. How can I possibly compete with that?"

"All I can say is, if you're his friend like you claim to be, then maybe you can help me figure out what's really going on. He's counting on us...*on me*...and I don't want to let him down."

That was the last straw. Sarah jumped off the bed, yanked open the closet door, and pulled a purple suitcase out from under a shelf of sweaters. Dust balls flew through the air, making her sneeze.

"Gesundheit," Mike grumbled.

She eyed him with more disdain than he felt she had a right to. Grabbing a dirty tee-shirt from the laundry basket, she wiped off the luggage and opened the lid.

"What are you doing, Sarah?"

"Packing."

He moved over to her and made a grab for her hands. She slapped him away and scooted around the bed, avoiding further contact. He followed close behind, reaching for her shoulder or arm or anything that might make her take pause.

"Stop it. Stop touching me. You want me to help you *figure out what's really going on*?" she spat, using air quotes around his own words. "One guess; Gary wins."

"I'm not letting you leave over something as stupid as this."

"Oh. So, now I'm stupid. Fine. Go. Go on your private manhunt for Gary Wolf. You'd do it whether I was here or not, so it really doesn't matter."

"Jesus, Sarah. Would you *stop*? Listen to yourself. Where the hell is all this coming from?"

Sarah reached down, picked up a pile of sweaters from the floor, and dropped it on the bed next to her suitcase. The top one flopped over showing three cheerful squirrels wearing scarves and holding acorns. They were dancing around a smiling snowman wearing a top hat.

"Why did you offer to pick them up tonight? They live down the street from us. What the hell is wrong with a taxi? Or they could have left their car in the airport parking lot. Gary was planning on doing that, you know. He told me. But then you offered your chauffer services even though you're the one who has to get up early. Hell, they can both sleep in 'til noon if they wanted."

"So what? I'm helping out a friend. I'm not forcing you to go to the airport with me, so why does any of this matter to you?"

"Because it's not just *this* time. It's not about picking them up tonight. It's not about going to the airport at midnight. It's about your obsession with having to be the hero. When he's fixing something at his house, you're the one that rushes over there. Not Jeff, his construction buddy, or Pete, the electrician from the office. It has to be *you*. Remember when he sprained his ankle last fall going down his porch steps? Who took him to the clinic? His *wife*? No, of course not. You actually left your client's Open House so you could drive him and you made Grace sit in the back seat of the car. *You* are not his wife, Mike. Stop acting like it."

"This is different."

"No, it's not. You have no proof that something is wrong. Computer glitches happen all the time; you know that. None of this would be happening if you let them take responsibility for their own actions. You and I could have had a nice dinner, maybe relaxed with a movie, and been in bed instead of dealing with all this crap."

"I-I don't know what to say here, Sarah. I really don't…,"

She sighed and let herself drop back onto the bed. Closing her eyes for just a moment helped her to clear her mind. It appeared as if she broke through to him. *Finally.*

She closed the lid of her suitcase, placed it on the floor next to the bed, and swung her legs out over the top of the blanket. Mike took the change in Sarah's position and demeanor as a cue to slide in next to her. He put his arm out so that she could rest her head on his shoulder. They lay together quietly for a few minutes, listening to each other breathe. With their eyes closed, they settled down into a peaceful state and held each other. There was a comfort in the fact that although they had fought, they came out stronger and closer on the other end.

That's how Sarah interpreted it.

Mike broke the silence. He looked at the clock on the nightstand.

"So, uh, we're good now, right? I'm glad that you got all that off your chest. I'll bet you feel a lot better now, huh? So, I think I'm gonna head back to the airport. Their flight doesn't get in for two hours, but I'm thinking that maybe I can find somebody else that knows their computer system better than that night supervisor. I'm assuming that you don't want to come with me."

Sarah blinked hard. She watched Mike get up from the bed, straighten his clothes in the mirror, and put his shoes back on.

"I shouldn't be back too late. If you don't want to wait up, that's fine. I know you have to work tomorrow, too."

He leaned over the bed and kissed her on the head.

"I'll see you soon, hon."

He gave her an awkward smile and left the room. She listened as he put his coat on, grabbed his keys, and opened the front door. A minute later, she heard the engine turn over. His tires crunched the snow underneath; leaving tracks in the driveway that would soon mingle with her own.

In what could only be described as an overwhelming silence, Sarah packed her suitcase and shut off all the lights in the house. She wasn't planning on coming back.

CHAPTER 26

Gary inched forward. He could no longer focus; his vision alternated between being a blurry haze and a watery cesspool. Every heart beat made his head throb worse than the time before, and if there had been anything left in his stomach, he would have relinquished it by now.

The fuzzy image next to him bandied back and forth between Grace and Kristy. Someone had recently mentioned the prospect of going home and it sounded wonderful. The mere mention of Bloomington was absolutely delicious; something he so desperately wanted and needed. It didn't matter which woman said it. All that mattered was that he was finally headed home and every step forward brought him that much closer to a glorious reality.

"This is it, Kristy? Just through the tunnel and we're there?"

Grace skirted to the side of the pit, moving far enough away that a frantic, grasping hand couldn't suddenly reach out and pull her along for the ride. She wasn't sure if he would survive the drop *again*, especially since he was blatantly unstable. In any case, she was beginning to rethink her initial diagnosis of a simple concussion; his symptoms appeared far worse now.

"Keep going, Gary. I'm right beside you. We're one step closer to Bloomington, just like we talked about earlier."

His left foot was only inches from the edge. *Why was he hesitating?*

"Gary, don't you want to go home?" Grace pressed. "Mike and Sarah are waiting for us. Don't you want to see them?"

He raised his head and turned toward her voice.

It didn't sound quite like Kristy. Grace? *Was that Grace? What was she doing here?*

The tunnel spun in front of him like an angry, black tornado. The air was stale. A metallic taste rose up from his gut to his throat and oozed its way into his mouth/ Bitterness. Caustic. Repulsive. It filled his pores and made him woozy. His right leg buckled under him as he stumbled toward Grace, his hands reaching out in the darkness, groping for something or someone to help steady his balance. Grace pressed herself up against the wall of the tunnel, moving just out of reach.

"Grace?"

She didn't answer. Instead, she waited and watched Gary's lumbering attempts to regain his footing. With a quick flash of her phone's light, she saw that his head and part of his face were covered in blood. In fact, his hair was one big mass of sweat, dirt, and blood.

"What? What was that? I saw light."

"My phone just went off. It's nothing."

"You have a light? Show me. I-I can't see."

"No more bars," she lied. "That flash was the final signal. But it's getting light outside, Gary. It's morning. That's why we need to keep going."

"Kristy? Is that you?"

This was taking far too long. She didn't want to take a chance that the tunnel might become bright enough for him to be able to distinguish the pit from a non-existent track. The sun probably wouldn't reach that far from the few high-placed windows along the lobby wall, but why dither with the details? She obviously had to encourage him more in order to make this happen.

"Yes, Gary. I'm right here. If you just go forward, we'll be out in a matter of minutes. I'm counting on you to lead the way."

"Oh, Kristy, thank God. I'm finally rid of that bitch Grace so it's just you an' me from now on."

With what little composure Gary could muster, he took two steps forward. On the third, his foot became airborne, sending him into a free-fall, straight down to the bottom of the pit. In the seconds it took him to make contact with the ground, his arms and legs flailed aimlessly like a broken windmill trying to right itself. Once his body converged with the earth, Grace heard enough snaps and cracks to let her know that broken bones were plentiful and that Gary wasn't going anywhere anytime soon.

The moment *after* Gary hit the ground, the jolt managed to smack him back into his dismal reality. Although physically, he was busted and mangled, he suddenly became very aware of where he was and with whom he had been speaking.

"Grace! Help, Grace!"

Cautiously, she stepped to the edge of the hole and peered over. She clicked on her phone and shone it down on Gary. He looked like a shadowy lump. She walked out of the tunnel and into the lobby. She wanted to see how bright it had become.

In the recesses of her mind, Grace thought about her church; the stained glass windows, the picturesque scenarios, the sacrificial scenes leading up to the death of her Lord. She envisioned the pews, lined up and empty, waiting to be filled with parishioners who would pray for redemption and forgiveness. She pictured the lectern and the pulpit; the very place where pardons would be granted and sinners might be cleansed. *But only if they believed strongly enough. Only if they dotted their 'i's' and crossed their 't's' and followed all the rules, would they be saved.*

A hideous and guttural laugh spewed from Grace's lips. If there was anyone among them that needed saving and repentance, it was Gary Wolf.

"Grace, please! I'm hurt!"

Gary tried to move his legs but it was like asking his body to do the impossible. The fall not only broke his right femur and both tibias, but shattered his pelvis. He still had a bit of mobility in his right arm and his head, but not enough to make a difference in his situation. Consciousness was also waning.

"I can hear you. I know you're up there."

The sun did its best to stream in through the inconsequential windows at the top of the wall. The beams made quick work of the ice that had covered them. The glass wept; icy tears slid down the small, thick panes.

Grace wondered if it would be possible to reach them, to knock them out and call for help. She looked skyward, realizing they were too far up even for her best effort. She had thought that the determination and confidence she felt after sleeping in the train *(or what she imagined was the train)*, would have given her the ability to conquer any physical barriers that stood in her way. She was mistaken.

"Grace? Where are you? I need you!"

She turned toward the tunnel-- toward her husband's voice. Everything about his tone and his utterances grated on her nerves and tore at her insides like a cheese shredder catching on a flap of skin. She needed time. She needed a plan. She needed for him to shut the hell up so she could have some peace and quiet to think.

Grace had enough of Gary and his incessant badgering for help.

CHAPTER 27

Mike pulled into the Central Illinois Regional Airport like a man on a mission. Even though he knew he had plenty of time to kill before the plane was due to arrive, he anticipated a number of possible scenarios, most of them culminating with apologies from the airline staff and free vouchers for airfare. But once he actually stepped inside and saw Jeffrey, the same squeaky-voiced newbie at the counter, his motivation and fervor plummeted. Instead, he walked through the building, located Gate 3, and checked the overhead screens to make sure that Flight 5632 was on time.

There were already a handful of other people in the waiting area. An elderly couple sharing one phone between them briefly studied the newcomer. Once they deemed Mike to be a non-threatening entity, they went back to their discussion involving whatever was on the tiny screen. The woman pointed to something that caused the man to raise his glasses off his nose and study more closely.

In the far corner near the windows, a young man sat quietly with his head down as he mindlessly fumbled with what looked like dog tags. Every now and then, he would stop and gaze outside toward the tarmac. Mike assumed the man was military. His burr flattop, jump boots and camouflage backpack felt like dead giveaways, but these days, Mike couldn't be sure of anyone's story. As a realtor, he learned rather quickly to ask questions and *never* assume when it came to a person's outward appearance.

The third group consisted of a middle aged couple with two kids. The older one, the daughter, was about fifteen; the younger boy couldn't have been much more than five. The parents were both glued to their own personal tablets, as was the daughter to her phone. The little boy must have thought his role in the family was to be the interrogator. His incessant and repetitious questions droned on, one after another, in rapid succession. His mom, dad, and sister were apparently masters at ignoring his constant babble.

Mike took a seat closest to the exit; a few seats away from the elderly couple. The man nodded silently to Mike before returning his attention back to his wife and their device. Mike noticed an insignia on the man's hat and smiled. The woman caught his reaction.

"There's no reason for that."

"Ma'am?" Mike asked.

"To be so judgmental. I saw you looking at Burl's hat."

"Oh, uh, I wasn't being...,"

"The Confederate flag is a symbol of pride. It's not racist. You young folks would do well to learn some history."

"I-uh...," Mike stammered.

"That's what the hell's wrong with people today," Burl added. "They don't see the problems for what they are. If you knew how things really were, you'd understand. G'damn liberals. Before you know it, they'll have *those kinds* taking over this country. Just a bunch of lazy, no good…,"

"Burl," his wife stopped him. "Watch your language. There's children about."

"Well, I hope you and your kind think long and hard about what you want for the future, mister."

"Look, I'm not trying to start anything here. All I'm doing is waiting for my friend's plane."

The man turned in his seat toward Mike in order to continue his tirade, but Mike was already up and moving away. The woman mumbled something to Burl, making him snort and turn his back in disgust. Words like liberal and race mixing made it to Mike's ears, but he wasn't in the mood for this type of confrontation.

He had to stay focused and alert for Gary's sake.

As time passed, more people trickled in. They found seats or stood around talking in small groups. Mike kept busy replaying his conversation with Sarah. He couldn't get over how she wasn't able to recognize the gravitas of the situation. Two of their best friends (well, at least one) could be in serious trouble. Didn't that trump any of her perceptions of jealousy? Surely by morning, she'd be able to recognize the pettiness of her arguments.

The little boy, who everyone within earshot had learned was named Tyler, bounded up to Mike and took the seat next to him. His red North Face jacket was unzipped and his wool hat was seconds away from falling off his head. He was sporting snow boots with cartoon characters who were in the midst of throwing snowballs at each other.

Tyler's red hair stuck out like a pile of straw underneath his hat. Mike guessed that it hadn't seen the business end of a comb or brush within the past twelve hours, at the *very* least.

"What's your name?" Tyler asked in an outdoor voice.

"Mike. What's yours?"

"Tyler Guisewhite. I live in Peoria. I'm five. My birthday was last week. Where do you live?"

"I live right here in Bloomington. Is that your family over there?"

"Yeah. That's my sister, Jeri. She's older than me. She's in high school. And that's my mom."

"Oh. Is that your dad?"

"No. He's my step-dad. My real dad's dead."

"Oh. I'm sorry to hear that, Tyler."

Tyler shrugged and looked down. Mike felt a pang of awkwardness; he wasn't sure how to proceed.

"So, um, Tyler? Is your family waiting for somebody?"

"Yeah. My Grampa. He's coming to stay with us 'cause gramma died."

"I see. Well, that should be pretty nice. Having your grandpa around, I mean."

Mike was feeling a little worse for wear. Poor kid had seen his share of death all before his first year of school. That's got to be tough for everyone involved. He glanced over at the family, all still glued to their devices.

"Why are *you* here?"

"Well," Mike started, "I'm here to pick up a friend and his wife. Their names are Gary and Grace. I'm going to give them a ride home so they don't have to wait for a taxi."

"Gary and Grace."

"Yes, that's right. They're friends of mine. I'll bet you would like them if you met them."

"No. I don't think so."

Mike laughed a bit. Kid's got a sense of humor. He wanted to make a snarky comment about Grace but realized that the reference would be lost on the five-year-old.

"You don't think so, do you? You don't think you would like them very much?"

"I don't think I'll meet them."

Mike raised his eyebrows and shifted in his seat.

"Oh, well, why is that? They'll probably be on the same flight as your grandpa. I think we're all waiting here for the same plane. They might even be sitting right next to him. What do you think about that?"

"I don't think so."

"Why not, Tyler? Why wouldn't they be sitting together?" Mike laughed at the presumptuous answer from the child.

Tyler raised his face to meet Mike's. The little boy's blue eyes were wide and glistened under the fluorescent lights of the terminal. His mouth drew up in a bow, just like in the poem, 'Twas the Night Before Christmas. He spoke without missing so much as a single beat.

"'Cause they're dead."

CHAPTER 28

2 December, 0730

The sun had brightened up the corridor and the entranceway of the Rain Bahnhof. Much of the ice that had coated the large glass windows near the mouth of the worm had given itself over to the penetrating warmth. Islets of cold pools lined the base of the windows, mixing with the dirt and grit from the floor, forming into a grey slurry of sorts. Meanwhile, Grace had been listening to Gary's sporadic cries for help and had enough of it. She held her purse against her body and leaned over the edge of the pit.

"Gary."

In his semi-conscious state, he strained to open his eyes and squinted toward the disembodied voice that floated somewhere above him. Bloodied, bruised, and broken, he was aware enough to sense the gnawing growl in his gut. Hunger hadn't necessarily been a top priority for him, but he was thirsty. He also understood that Grace couldn't get him out of the hole by herself, but he hung on to a thread of hope that outside help was on the way.

At this point, Gary just didn't want to be left alone. If that meant Grace would have to perch on the edge of the pit and wait with him until someone else arrived, then that's what he expected her to do.

"Grace? Where were you? Where'd you go?"

"I was checking out the lobby. I remembered that there were windows, but I guess I didn't realize how small they were. And high...way too high. You do realize that I can't get you out of there on my own."

"I-I know. I just wanted to know that you're close by."

"Where the hell else would I be right now?"

"I think I broke my legs...everything hurts. I need to get to a hospital."

"I imagine you do, Gary."

"What time is it?"

"Just before eight."

"In the morning?"

"Yes. In the morning. Can you see anything down there? It's actually not too horrible up here. The sun's up and there's some light coming in from the corridor."

Gary tried moving but the effort made his head swim. Nausea washed over his body and he turned his head just in time to empty his gut. There wasn't much; mostly acid and bile. His esophagus and throat stung from the trouble.

"That doesn't sound good," Grace tossed off.

As Gary coughed and sputtered, Grace was struck by an odd grinding noise coming from the other side of the wall. She went over to the windows in the corridor and rubbed her hands against the glass, but the melted ice only served to make the windows blurry. It was like trying to see through a sheet of wet plastic wrap. She pounded on them just in case someone was there, but it became very clear that her fists were no match for the sound of the machinery.

The grinding was now accompanied by what sounded like a cacophony of chainsaws. She couldn't be sure exactly *what* was taking place, but there was definitely *something* going on directly outside the building.

"Kristy! I need you! Where did you go?" Gary called out from the pit.

Grace stepped away from the windows. Whatever was happening had caused the building and the floor to shake. The intense vibrations were strong enough to loosen snowy white particles from the ceiling of the lobby as well as the corridor. The microscopic bits rained down on top of her.

She opened her arms with a wide and welcoming spread, capturing as much as she could; her eyes and mouth open, taking every molecule in by any means possible. She believed that every fragment and sliver was a loving touch to her parched and desolate soul. This sacrilegious integration quenched her hunger and gave her a strength that had been unattainable with Gary.

A low rumble radiated through the station, culminating with a shockwave that rang out and poured into the tunnel. A steady beat of tremors came up through the ground. They dislodged the infrastructure of the pit and unearthed what had been buried for months.

Fine, powdery earth and grit were shaken loose and cascaded to the ground. It surrounded him like a wreath. The dirt was of little concern, however. What troubled Gary was the fact that these tremors were coming from somewhere out in the world, somewhere beyond his reach. And whatever was buried beneath the tunnel and in the walls of the pit was coming home to roost.

A partially decomposed torso covered in gangly shreds of a dress shirt had rolled free from one of the dirt walls and came to rest three feet from where he lay. What was once clean, pressed, and white was now matted and discolored by a mix of dirt, blood, and sinew. The lower half of a human leg stuck out from the far wall of the pit in a comedic gesture, pointing accusatorily at Gary, mocking him with its own broken tibia. A jawbone jutted out from another section of the wall. A few skulls tumbled and broke upon landing; the teeth scattering like dice on a craps table. Shards of ribs and chipped vertebrae shook free from their mud-coated nesting spots and joined the rest of the hellacious atrocities at the bottom of the hole. A few pairs of shoes, some still carrying what remained of their owners' feet, were also freed by the tumult. Thanks to Grace shining her phone over the edge, supposedly to check on him, Gary was able to see every ghoulish nightmare.

His addled brain was reeling. He tried to rationalize the horrors around him by clinging to a shred of distorted reality.

"Kristy?! Is this an earthquake? Get me out of here! Please!"

Grace clicked the light off and stepped back into the lobby. The stream of human particles and dust continued to wash over her in a repulsive and vile state of communion. When she finally felt as if she had been satiated, she once again stepped to the pit's edge and shouted down to Gary.

"Kristy isn't here."

"I-I don't...understand. She was here a minute ago. I was talking to her."

"I'm *Grace*, your wife. Kristy was never here."

"Grace? I-I I'm confused."

He was beyond delusional now.

"Where am I?" he yelled. "Who are you?"

She switched her phone on again and held it over the side of the hole. He started to hallucinate moments before his body began to seize.

"*Mannequins! There's mannequins down here*!"

"Those aren't mannequins, Gary."

A severed head rolled down from the side of the wall and landed in front of his face. Gary didn't see the dirt-covered skull with the chipped teeth and the dented jaw. Gary saw something else. In what was left of his mind, he saw the head of his office lover, Kristy.

Her head stared back at him with big green eyes, pouty lips, and caked-on make-up. Her hair was stringy and matted and streaked with blood. Her mouth was open just enough for him to see a grey-green tongue protrude in a wormlike fashion. Her neck appeared to have been sawed off by a dull chainsaw; the skin at the bottom was shredded and uneven.

Gary screamed with every fiber and cell in his being while Grace squatted at the edge of the pit and laughed maniacally.

CHAPTER 29

Mike's eyes darted around the waiting area, seeing if anyone had overheard the bizarre exchange between him and this mysterious child. When no one even so much as glanced in their general direction, Mike turned his attention back to Tyler. He cleared his throat and fidgeted in his seat. How could a little kid make a forty-two year old man so uncomfortable?

"Tyler, why...why would you say such a thing?"

"'Cause it's true," he said and slid off the chair onto his feet. His boots squeaked when they hit the floor.

"Wait a minute. Don't go just yet. I want to know why you think that my friends are hurt. Because they're *not*, you know. It's not like what happened to your grandma."

"I don't fib."

"I-I'm not saying that do you, buddy." Mike couldn't believe he was having a philosophical dialogue with a five year old. "I just want to know why you would say something like that."

"I told you already. 'Cause it's true. Bye."

The boy gave Mike an apathetic wave and trundled over to his parents and sister who hadn't looked up yet. Tyler crawled up onto his mom's lap, jammed his thumb into his mouth, and intentionally avoided any further eye contact with Mike.

A muffled announcement came over the loud speaker which startled everyone at Gate 3. The voice sounded female; Mike wondered if it was the lovely Kelly Sparks with whom he had spoken to earlier. The flight, arrival time, and gate number were clear enough. Everyone moved closer to the door, after having gathered up their belongings, and strained to see the aircraft approaching the tarmac. Everyone, that is, except Mike.

He purposefully hung back. He wanted to be certain that he laid eyes on every person who stepped off the small plane and entered the airport. If he was *in* the crowd, he might miss someone, and that wasn't going to be good enough tonight. It was up to him to make sure his friends made it *all the way home* safely, regardless of what Sarah thought about the situation.

The small plane coasted, touched down, and came to a stop. As the engines winded down, a sense of anxiousness and energy became almost palpable within the terminal. Once the lights came on inside the plane, a flurry of activity could be seen from the windows; passengers collecting items from the overhead compartments, chatting with seatmates, accessing their phones.

Tyler was already by the door, waving and shouting for his grandpa. His parents stood behind him, devices turned off for the time being. His sister was still seated, eyes glued to her own screen, bored by the family's display of emotions. Whatever she was looking at was making her smile in a way her parents and brother couldn't possibly understand. *They were obviously too lame to be as cool as she was.*

There was the usual commotion inside the plane before the ramp was lowered. A young flight attendant stood next to the exit and offered her hand for those needing support as they descended to the first step. Another attendant waited at the bottom in order to provide further assistance; a few passengers took them up on the offer.

As people walked through the doors of the airport, they were greeted by tired but happy family or friends. A few continued past the waiting area and headed to the luggage carousel. Others were already on their cell phones making plans involving cabs or hotel reservations.

Tyler's grandfather ambled through the doors; a plastic Osco bag in one hand and a wooden cane in the other. His family gathered and fussed around him, talking and asking questions all at once. Even Tyler's sister was in the fray now, happy to see her grandpa and anxious to show him something on her phone that she thought was *hilarious*.

Mike looked away from the entrance long enough to watch Tyler leave with his family. The boy never looked back.

Eventually, all the other passengers had either met with people or collected their bags and left the terminal, including the quiet military man. Mike remained vigilant; he stood by the Gate 3 service desk and kept an eye on the door for any stragglers.

It was close to 12:20 by the time the flight crew and staff entered the building.

"Uh, excuse me. Where are the rest of the passengers? My friends are supposed to be on this flight."

"Everyone's been through, sir. The plane's empty. This was the final flight of the night for us," a man from the group said. He was carrying two extremely large flashlights.

"But my friends were on there. Are you sure there's no one left?"

"Everyone's de-boarded the plane. There's no one else out there. We're it."

"That can't be. They were scheduled to be home tonight. Gary and Grace Wolf."

"Maybe check with the ticket counter? Sorry, but there's no one else on that plane."

The flashlight man caught up to the rest of his group just before they filed into a door labeled STAFF ONLY.

Mike stood alone in the waiting area, dumbfounded. *What the hell was he supposed to do now?* He checked his phone for messages but there were none. He wondered if Sarah had heard anything on her end and thought about calling her, but decided not to push his luck.

"No," he whispered. "That won't help anything."

Instead, he hustled to the ticket counter just in time to see the night manager engaged in what appeared to be closing procedures.

"Ma'am, I need your help. My friends weren't on the plane and I can't get a hold of them. Can you help me find them? I don't know what to do."

Kelly Sparks, the woman with the bun pulled too tight looked up. When she saw Mike, she lowered her glasses. A sense of recognition washed over her face.

"I think we've already had this discussion if I'm not mistaken. Have you checked with the ground crew? They're the ones who handle…,"

He cut her off in mid-sentence. He didn't have time to play games.

"No. Don't even," he held up his hand. "I want you…no, I *need* you to get on your computer and check the manifest or guest list or whatever the hell you guys call it and tell me where my friend is. I don't care how long it takes. And if you can't or won't, then I suggest you find someone who can and who will."

The woman pushed her glasses back against the bridge of her nose. Her demeanor immediately shifted; she became indignant. Kelly Sparks switched the computer off, threw a pile of luggage tags into a partially open drawer under the counter, and slammed it shut. She paused an extra beat before responding to Mike's demands.

"This counter is closed. Our last flight has come through and every person on our manifest has been accounted for. If your friends changed their plans or flight schedules, then take it up with them. As far as Blue Airways is concerned, we've showed you what *our* records have regarding the status of your friends. If you refuse to check with the ground crew, there's nothing more I can do for you. Good night."

"Gary Wolf is not dead!" Mike shouted. His voice echoed through the terminal, drawing the attention of assorted TSAs and a few passengers who hadn't left the building yet.

"Lower your voice, please," Kelly whispered. "Or do I need to contact security?"

"Is there a problem here?" A beefy TSA agent wearing clothes one size too small asked.

"No, I don't think so. *Is there a problem here?*" she pointedly asked Mike.

"Yes, there's a big problem. This lady is telling me that my friend came home in a box and I'm calling bullshit on that. So, yeah, we have a problem."

The TSA man nodded to Kelly and led Mike away from the counter. Ms. Sparks looked relieved and exhausted and ducked into another doorway marked STAFF ONLY as fast as she could.

"Look, sir. I don't know the whole story, but let's go down to the shipping bay and find out what's going on. Will you do that with me?"

Mike agreed. *What choice did he have?* Without a word, he followed the security agent down a set of stairs, through two metal doors, and down a maze of hallways located underneath the airport. He was a little surprised by this *city under a city* layout. It reminded him of an article he read about the underground design used by Disney; how a whole world can exist right under people's feet without them having a clue.

Eventually, they entered a large area that resembled a mail room. Bays of gravity roller conveyor machines busily whirred, providing bumpy rides for a variety of boxes and containers that had come off the planes during the evening. A handful of workers dressed in jet blue coveralls with matching baseball caps ran back and forth between enormous burlap carts and the conveyor belts. A man who was dressed in a heavy blue oxford shirt and brown Dockers sat behind a glass window at a desk overseeing the hive of activity.

He was almost bald, but it didn't stop him from proudly displaying a sad looking comb-over. His office didn't have pictures of a wife or kids. Instead, framed photos of him dressed as various Star Trek characters attending multiple Comic-Cons adorned his desk. There was a banner taped over his computer saying: *Lordy, Lordy, Look (Dr.) Who is 40*. On a small bookcase behind his chair were file folders, airport binders, and a collection of Dungeon Master Rules and Guidebooks. A large and very used-looking plastic bag of colorful 8, 12, and 20-siders perched next to them. His name tag said John Donovan, Supervisor.

"Hey, John."

"Howdy, Justin. What brings you down to the bowels of the building tonight?"

"Got a guest here that's looking for someone. Kelly thought they might be down here."

John stepped around his desk and met the two men just outside of the office doorway. He was barely 5'6 and that was with one and a half inch heels on his boots. The folded-up cuffs of his pants were worn and dirty from having been repeatedly stepped on and dragged over the floor.

"Down here? If they were down here that would only mean one thing."

"Yeah, we know. Just checking up on her suggestion."

Mike could no longer restrain himself. He didn't like the situation and he didn't care for this John character. It felt like no one was taking this as seriously as they should have been.

"Look. John?"

"Mr. Donovan."

Mike couldn't help but roll his eyes. The posturing and alpha-male games grated on his nerves.

"John. Your night manager, Kelly, told me one thing, but my intuition tells me another. I can't get a hold of my friend and he didn't get off the plane he was supposed to be on tonight. So now I'm being led here and there because no one upstairs will help me."

John looked toward Justin for clarification. The TSA shrugged, shook his head, and gestured to Mike.

"Did you get any…uh, remains, anytime today?"

"Nope." John Donovan crossed his arms over his balloon-like gut.

"What? Just like that? You don't check? You don't have a list? You don't even bother with talking to your workers to see if they've come across anything during their shifts? What kind of crap is this?"

"Excuse me, mister…uh…,"

"Mike."

"Well, excuse *me*, Mike, but you don't have to tell me how to do my job. If there was a body on board any one of our aircraft, there's a shitload of procedures and regulations that we'd have to follow. I'm not gonna bore you with all the details and arrangements that go into body transport, but let me assure you that if your friend was due to arrive in a box, I'd know about it. I've been here for almost seven hours and nothing like that, paperwork or otherwise, has come across my desk."

"But the manager said…,"

"I don't care what they said upstairs. The programs they use up there are pieces of shit. Hell, they might as well be using an Apple II word processor and dot matrix."

Justin thought John's comment was funny as shit. Mike gave him a dirty look before responding to the supervisor.

"Well, you tell me, John, who am I supposed to believe? The night manager or some glorified shipping clerk who works in a basement on the midnight shift?"

John's face looked like it had been slapped with a wet glove. He stepped toe to toe with Mike, tilted his head back, and looked right up into the man's nostrils. He pointed a stubby, nail-bitten finger toward his face and furrowed his brow.

"I am the supervisor here. I'm in charge of everything that goes on in this room, and for your information, I am far from *clerk* status. I don't need to put up with your attitude, accusations, or insults. I already told you. Your friend is not down here. No *body* came through today. At all. Period. Infinito. Now please leave. Justin, will you escort this guy out of here before I really get pissed? I've got real work to do."

"Sure, John. C'mon, sir, let's go."

The TSA went to grab Mike's arm, but he yanked it away before the man could get a hold of him. Grudgingly, he followed Justin back through the winding hallways and passages until they reached the lobby of the airport.

Kelly Sparks, the ground crew, and the other workers had all left. A few scattered security agents were busy checking locks on gates and walking the inside perimeter.

"Sorry we couldn't find your friend, sir, but you'll have to leave the terminal now. We need to finish locking up."

"Unbelievable," Mike muttered. "Fine, I'm going. You don't need to walk me to my car. I think I can handle that by myself."

Justin nodded and unlocked a door off of the main lobby that led to the parking lot. Mike zipped up his coat and put his gloves back on before heading to his lone car in Aisle D. A cold gust of wind hit him in the face, but he didn't bother to cover his nose and mouth with the scarf that hung around his neck.

The icy chill felt good; *reviving*.

He drove home with the windows rolled down and the radio off.

CHAPTER 30

The wheels of the Prius had barely come to stop before Mike threw the car into Park and had the door open. He practically leapt from the driver's seat and tore into the house; key at the ready to unlock the front door. One arm was already out of his coat sleeve while the other was checking his phone for messages that might have come through in the interim. But there was nothing to see; not a single text or call. He shook his other arm loose and let the jacket fall to the floor.

Mike tried Gary's number. The phone didn't ring at all. Instead, a computerized voice stated that the number was temporarily out of service. He stared blankly at the device in his hand and determined it was time to get desperate. He called Grace's number and waited while it rang, here too, no one answered.

"Dammit!"

A sinking feeling of desperation churned in his gut. He slammed his phone down on the kitchen counter and let out a string of expletives that would make the salty and vulgar proud.

"Oh, shit," he whispered, realizing that he might have woken Sarah by his outburst and slapped a hand over his mouth.

He tip-toed quietly into the living room, turning a few lights on along the way, and removed his shoes. He shot a glance down the hallway to see if his outburst woke his wife. When she didn't appear, he stretched out on the couch and closed his eyes. He needed to *think*. Better yet, he needed to *act.*

How could two people just disappear without a trace?

The only reasonable thing left to do was to contact the police. But from where? *Germany* or *Bloomington?* And what would he possibly say to make them understand the severity of the situation? Gary and Grace were adults; they didn't have to clear anything with Mike. What if they headed to France? What if they booked a flight with a different airline at the last minute?

While it was true that Gary had given him their schedule, their itinerary wasn't written in stone. Maybe they were having such a great time that they decided to extend the trip for a few days. It was their belated honeymoon, after all. Who wouldn't want to jet-set around Europe if you had the chance and the financial means to do so?

But if that *were* the case, why didn't Gary let him know? Gary Wolf had always been a conscientious guy, someone who was organized and followed a plan. If something had changed or if they no longer needed a ride for any reason, Mike would have been notified. No, something was wrong. It wasn't like Gary, or Grace for that matter, to leave someone hanging after plans had been made.

Even if the cops told him that he was overreacting, at least he would have tried. He was convinced; contacting the police was the right thing…the *only* thing…left to do.

It was a quarter to one in the morning. He resigned himself to the fact that getting a decent night's sleep was already out of the question. And, he supposed, it would wise to clue Sarah in as to what was happening; especially if the cops sent a squad car to the house.

"She's not going to like this," he muttered. "Like a band-aid. Tell her quick and it'll hurt a lot less."

A quiet laugh escaped his lips. He yawned and stretched as he rose from the couch. With just a hint of hesitation, he headed down the dark hallway to the master bedroom.

◆ ◆ ◆

Mike turned the knob as gently as he could and entered the room. It was dark as pitch; not a hint of moonlight shone through the blinds as it had on previous nights. A stale mustiness hung in the air that he hadn't noticed before. He sniffed around, trying to place the peculiar scent. It was familiar but his mind was too occupied to recognize it.

He felt his way past the dresser to the short nightstand before reaching Sarah's side of the bed. He leaned over, extending his arm. Instead of touching her shoulder, his hand fell flat onto the bedspread.

"Sarah?" he whispered.

He stretched over toward his side of the bed, playing a sort of blind man's bluff with the blankets.

"Sarah?"

He turned on the little gold lamp that sat squarely in the middle of her bedside table, squinting until his eyes adjusted to the change.

"Sarah."

Mothballs.

That was the smell that had welcomed him into their bedroom. He and Sarah kept a few mothballs in their suitcases to prevent hungry moths from feasting on their Samsonite when not in use. Since they hadn't taken a trip for over three months, there was only one reason for such an odor to permeate the room *now*.

"Dammit, Sarah! What did you *do*?"

Mike rustled through her side of the closet only to discover an empty space where her suitcase had been. A few lonely pieces of white tissue paper, hurriedly discarded in what appeared to be a rushed job of packing, lay on the carpet. Upon further inspection, he noticed the empty hangers, the missing piles of clothes, and a few dresser drawers partially open. A lone sock hung over the lip of the top drawer like a wagging tongue taunting onlookers.

"Great! That's just great," he bellowed. "Of all nights, you pick *this* one to make some point? Why are you doing this to me?"

He flew out of the bedroom, stomped down the hall, and grabbed his phone. He punched in her number with abandon, fat fingering the buttons, forcing him to redial. He listened, waited, and heard it go to message.

"Jesus, Sarah, *really*? I can't believe you'd actually take it this far."

He tried a few more times, only to get the same result. He flung the phone into the couch where it once again bounced off the cushions and landed on the floor. He let out a guttural growl and fell onto the sofa out of frustration. He put his hands over his face and attempted to catch his breath. An old VHS tape for meditation that Sarah had used in the past flashed through his mind. The leotard-clad instructor had spoke about calming breaths. He wondered if they still owned that video.

"Think, damn it. Stay focused," he told himself. "Where the hell would she go at this hour? *With her suitcase?"*

He scrolled through a list of her friends in his head. He could text them, but it was already so late. He also didn't think that her friends would appreciate the theatrics. If she really had the gumption to pack up and leave, there had already been enough drama tonight at *somebody's* house.

"What if they're all together? What if they planned this whole thing and all three of them ran off together? Wouldn't that be a real kick in the head?"

An awkward laugh escaped from his lips which caught him by surprise. The awkward outburst made him self-conscious. He cringed and scanned the empty living room as if suddenly breaking a code of silence. He quickly dismissed the idea of his wife and his best friend scheming behind his back.

"Don't. Don't be a fool," he mumbled. "You gotta keep it together, man."

He picked his phone up off the floor and texted his wife.

Where are you? Got home, you're gone. I'm worried. Please contact me ASAP. Gary and Grace still missing. Love M

He read it over before hitting send. Should he have mentioned Gary? Would that keep her from responding?

"Fuck it."

He hit send and then typed a message to Gary.

Where are you? Was at the airport – did I miss u? R U staying in Germany? Please message or call me.

He laid the phone on the arm of the couch and went into the kitchen. If there was ever a time to have a drink, it was now. He opened the refrigerator and looked at the bottle of Pinot that had been chilling for dinner.

"No. This night calls for the hard stuff."

He opened one of the cabinets and removed a bottle of Crown Royal from the top shelf. With a glass from the counter in one hand, he reached into the freezer and pulled out a handful of ice cubes with the other. He had no interest in making a proper cocktail; this was all about getting drunk as quickly as possible. In his haste, Mike's hands trembled, spilling the whisky over the lip of the glass. The liquid pooled over the counter and dribbled down the front of the cabinets and on to his clothes.

"Shit."

He blotted at his shirt and pants with a dish towel before taking a sip. He mumbled something about being thankful that it wasn't red wine. He took everything into the living room and placed the bottle and glass on the coffee table. He picked up the phone with every intention of calling the police, but set it down again.

The Crown Royal bottle was so regal. *So inviting*. It would make everything better.

He grasped the glass in his hands, drained his drink, and poured again. He repeated the cycle until the crown was conquered. *Another dead soldier.* Wasn't that what people said when they polished off a bottle of alcohol?

It was 1:30am when Mike finally got up the courage to call Bloomington's Finest.

CHAPTER 31

By the time the two Bloomington Police officers knocked on the door, Mike was well past the happy, friendly state of drunkenness. Rather, he was firmly planted in a state of confusion and not that far away from peering into the mouth of stupor.

"Come in. Please," he said, holding the front door open, allowing the uniformed men entrance.

"Sir, are you the one who called about a missing person?"

"*Two* people. *Two* people are missing; my wife and my best friend. Actually, it's three. My best friend's wife is missing, too." He held up two fingers from one hand and a single digit from the other.

The officers shot each other a look. *That kind of look*. The one they had shared during other domestic calls when drinking had obviously been a part of the scenario. The younger man pulled a small notebook and pencil from his shirt pocket and began taking notes while the older officer took the lead.

"Why don't we all have a seat and you can tell us what's been going on tonight, alright?"

Mike nodded and stumbled into the La-Z-Boy recliner.

"Have you been drinking tonight, sir?"

"I just had one. I was worried. I didn't know what else to do."

"*One* glass? Are you certain about that?"

"One or two. I don't remember," Mike slurred. "I was upset."

The officers noted the empty bottle on the table. Observations were scribbled down.

"Might *that* have something to do with the missing persons?"

Mike fidgeted and tried to stand but couldn't get his legs to cooperate. He grabbed for the arm of the couch in order to steady himself, but miscalculated. The older officer guided him back to the La-Z-Boy before taking his own seat again.

"Sir, why don't you just sit there and talk to us. Nobody needs to go anywhere at the moment. Can you stay in your chair and help us out?"

"I want you to know that *I* had nothing to do with *their* disappearances," Mike said. He pushed himself further back until the chair reclined. "I'll tell you exactly what happened and you'll see that *my drinking* has nothing to do with anything."

He gestured to the empty bottle, drained the last few watered down drops from the glass, and took an overly dramatic breath before he explained everything he knew about Gary and Grace. Halfway through his story about his wife's vanishing act, the young officer stopped him.

"Hold on for a second. This Gary and Grace Wolf are in Germany. Is that correct?"

"Yesss," Mike slurred. He was sleepy and regretted having called the police. *Couldn't they just leave and forget the whole thing?*

"So, we're talking about a couple on their honeymoon…,"

"B'lated honeymoon."

"Belated, okay. They're in Germany, though. And your wife's not with them."

"No. She was supposed to be in bed."

"You and your wife had a fight before you went to the airport."

"Well…yeah…but…,"

"Were you drinking before you went there?"

"No, of course not."

"But you came home and started drinking."

"Yeah…but what does that…,"

"So, you didn't call any of your wife's friends or relatives when you realized that she wasn't here."

"No… it was late."

The officers looked at each other and nodded. They stood and gathered their things. The older man put his hand on Mike's shoulder.

"No. No need to get up."

Mike had the sinking sensation that he was about to be disciplined by two disapproving parents. He raised his head as slowly as possible. He was a mess. A glassy-eyed, sweaty and pale mess. His head ached and his gut felt full and bloated. If he didn't puke in the next *five* minutes, he'd surely pass out in the next *four*.

"Mr. Waverly, I think we have everything we need. My suggestion for you is to get some sleep and give her friends a call in the morning. That is, if she doesn't come home before then. It sounds you two had a bad fight. But in our experience, spouses *do* calm down. Usually by the next day, everybody's minds are a little clearer."

"What about Gary?"

"Well, to be honest, there's not much we can do. Obviously, we have no jurisdiction outside of McLean County, let alone Germany. But if this Mr. and Mrs. Wolf are responsible people like you say they are, this whole thing is probably a breakdown of communication on either their end or yours. It's very likely that they've changed their plans and for whatever reason, the message just didn't reach you."

Mike stared at the blurry man standing before him. The alcohol was playing havoc with his eyesight. Back in his college days, he could polish off a twelve pack and not even blink twice; these days were painfully different. The contents of his stomach were creeping their way back up his esophagus and he silently prayed that he would be alone when his guttural hell broke loose.

"You know," the younger officer said, "this whole thing is probably just a glitch in the computer system's mainframe. That message *you* got and the one at the *airport*? Probably connected. I wouldn't worry about it; these things happen all the time. Computers go haywire on you without even trying."

Mike nodded to the men. It was all he could do to keep from letting the internal pressure explode.

"Here's my card," the older officer said. "If you think of anything else, give us a call, okay?"

They left the house with little fanfare, leaving Mike alone with his personal demons. The house screamed with a dead silence, save for the clock above the mantel in the living room.

The moment he heard the cruiser pull away, he lunged out of the La-Z-boy and tore down the hall to the bathroom in order to unload that which could no longer be contained.

◆ ◆ ◆

Mike didn't remember passing out; he had lost track of the past ninety minutes. Nauseating waves of unease and dizziness swept over him like the swell of the ocean at high tide. His eyes were dry and irritated, even though they had been shut the entire time. His ears were being assaulted by a disembodied high-pitched buzz.

A cold sweat covered his body like a glaze. His hands trembled as he fumbled with the shower curtain, pushing it away as he kneeled over the side of the tub. The toilet, he incorrectly assumed, was too small a target for his projectile vomit. Dry heaves followed close behind, wrenching him back and forth across the low white porcelain wall. When he was emptied of all spirits, his let his body slump back to the bathroom floor. He lay there, quivering, for the better part of an hour.

Mike didn't realize how drinking a few glasses of whisky could have affected him so badly. He had always been a moderate, social drinker. He knew his limitations and he rarely had *one too many*, even when he and Sarah attended the after-hours office parties. Having a few glasses of wine with dinner was routine for them. How could he have let it get *this* out of hand? No wonder the police weren't taking him seriously. He must have looked like a complete fool.

As he tried to stand, using the towel rack for support, he admonished himself for his lack of common sense. What was he thinking by downing almost half a bottle of Crown Royal? He knew better than to engage in this stupid frat-boy behavior. Why even call the police? Pulling a stunt like that was only putting him behind the eight ball. *He knew better. Where the hell were his priorities?*

With a newfound rage and frustration borne in his belly and his brain, Mike gave up on his feeble attempts to stand, which weren't going very well, and crawled on his hands and knees to the den. He clumsily clambered up onto the chair and switched the computer on.

"I'm not giving up, you piece of shit. You are not going to win this one."

Covering much of the same ground as he had before, he searched site after site, combed through old emails, and repeatedly refreshed the same pages. When the screen turned blue and showed an error message, he pounded his fists on the keyboard and swore at the screen. The terminal blinked on and off again in response to all the keys being hit. Beeps and buzzes choked out in an eerie symphony.

Beads of perspiration flew from Mike's face and his eyes were wide and bloodshot. His hair was spiked in unnatural peaks and his hands reddened from beating on the desk out of blind desperation.

"You fucking piece of shit! What's wrong with you? Tell me what I need to know!"

He grabbed the monitor with both hands and shook it within an inch of his face, screaming the entire time.

"G'damn piece of garbage! I hate you! I hate you, you cocksucking computer. I've had it!"

Mike ripped the monitor off the desk which sent cords and connection wires flying. Sparks sizzled and flashed as cables tore away from their docking points. He spun around in a dizzying whirl and threw the monitor across the room, smashing it into the far wall. In the next moment, he picked up the computer and slammed it onto the desk right where the monitor had been.

In a state of madness, he scanned the room, looking for a tool in order to knock some sense into the machine. The shiny glint from one of the fireplace pokers caught his eye. Without entertaining any rational thought or foresight on the matter, he picked up the implement, squeezed his hands into a death grip around the base, and swung the poker up and over his head.

In one fell swoop, he smashed it down on the computer over and over again, screaming with each blow, cursing each time he struck it. After finally breaking through the hard plastic case, the central processing unit of the computer was exposed. It taunted him with its technological components.

"You fuckin' piece of shit! I hate you! Die, you son of a bitch, die!!"

Again and again, Mike brought the poker down as hard as he could, punctuating each strike with a cuss word. Spittle flew from his lips and sweat dripped down from his brow. Enraged and driven with such intense anger, he didn't realize that the computer was still plugged in.

On the twelfth strike, the head of the poker made contact with just the right mechanism inside the computer's guts to send a current of electricity up through the tool and into Mike's body. At the same moment, an open bottle of water that had been sitting next to the mouse pad since earlier in the day, tipped over and spilled its contents. In a matter of seconds, the water seeped directly into and underneath the battered machine.

The unholy trio of water, electricity, and human being, collided.

There was an audible *pop* a single moment before the room lit up in a dazzling, ghostly glow. The illumination held on long enough before sparking and fading to black, taking out the rest of the lights in the house with it.

Sarah wasn't aware of it yet, but she no longer had a need to hire a lawyer and file for separation.

Mike lay unresponsive on the ground, only a yard away from his cell phone. The path of the electrical current which hadn't yet found an exit, continued to race through his body. Ultimately, it was either the ventricular fibrillation *or* the respiratory arrest which was the cause of his demise. The final decision would be determined by emergency room physicians in the days that followed.

CHAPTER 32

Gary's screams ultimately succumbed to the strain on his vocal cords and finally gave out. The quality of his voice that once commanded strength had devolved into a scratchy, whispery weakness. As far as Grace knew, he had either fallen asleep or slipped into unconsciousness. But if the past thirty minutes were any indication, she believed that his complaints and hallucinations would start up again *if and when* he came to.

"You're only hurting yourself, you know," Grace called down, her legs draped over the edge of the pit. "If you save your voice, you might be able to call for help when they open the doors."

"Who…who's coming?" Gary choked out in a raspy grate.

"I don't know, but it won't be long now. Mike and Sarah probably got a hold of the police since we weren't on the plane. Knowing them, they'll have the search dogs sniffing around the whole town by now. Especially for *you*."

Gary found it impossible to get a bead on what Grace was telling him. He was too disoriented. The hemorrhage in his brain kept him from fully comprehending his part in the dialogue.

"How? I-I don't understand...,"

"We didn't get on the plane, Gary. Airlines have records of that stuff. If they went to the airport to pick us up and we never showed, they'd have to figure out that something went wrong somewhere."

"But...finding us...how?"

Grace thought for a moment. *How indeed?* Even if they contacted the *right* train station, there would be no information as to their whereabouts since they never arrived. No one in either country knew that they were trapped in the *wrong* terminal.

"Good point, Gary. No one *would* ever think to look for us in here."

A moment of silent contemplation sat with each of them.

The sun was doing its best to warm the inside of the dead terminal. The ice that had coated the windows had melted, leaving snail-like trails behind. Grace could hear quite a bit of commotion from the outside and it made her confident that help was only minutes away. If she could detect the noise from *within* the tunnel, they were certainly as good as rescued. If they weren't coming through the side door, they'd be walking down the corridor from the main entrance any time now.

In the moments leading up to their rescue, Grace thought about Bloomington, Illinois; about her house and her life as she knew it *before* the trip. She was done tolerating Gary's bullshit. Everything was going to be *different* when they got home. No more affairs with Kristy or whoever was flavor-of-the-month anymore. Gary's name would be removed from all of her bank accounts, credit cards, and will.

Since the house was already in her name, that paperwork could stand. But she would be damned if he was going to benefit from her tax returns again. There would be lawyers and mountains of paperwork to deal with, but in the end it would all be worth it. She was sick and tired of being exploited.

Why should I even bother staying married to him? It's obvious that he doesn't love me...if he ever did in the first place. It was only about money. My money and his need for greed. I'd be so much better off without him.

"Gary?"

A raggedy thought bubble popped over his head when Grace broke the silence. He was in the midst of forcing two thoughts together. The first was something about Kristy – something about her body pressed up against his; lips touching, legs intertwined. How would that happen now? What if he came out of this paralyzed from the waist down or worse yet, *lost* one of his legs? Would she still want him?

The second thought revolved around Grace. How did she fit into the picture? Was she a part of his picture after all? Nevertheless, she was still his wife and there would be a quagmire of messy legal ties. But maybe, after living through this nightmare, he could be free of her. Maybe she wouldn't want to be married to him once this was over.

But what about money? That was important. He needed Grace. He needed Grace's *money*.

"Gary? Can you hear me?"

More drilling outside. This time, it was accompanied by what sounded like jackhammers. Grace shouted over the ruckus to be heard.

"Gary!"

It was too surreal. Gary wasn't sure if Grace was actually yelling at him or if this was some kind of tumultuous dream. The vibrations coming up from the ground caused more dirt and more groundswell to shift and fill up the inside the pit. More disembodied skulls and pieces of bones dislodged, tumbling from what was once their makeshift crypt and joining the other lost souls. The hole looked like a macabre playground for ghoulish children.

In order to escape this grotesque scenario, Gary hoisted himself back onto his elbows and tried pulling himself away from the crater's center, but he didn't get far. The movement only served to send sharp waves of pain through his body. He tried to muffle his weakened cries, but ended up passing out from the pain.

"Gary, can you hear me?"

No response.

"Well, whether you can or not, I've come to a decision. I want a divorce. I don't need you anymore. I am done with your lying and cheating and having your hands all over my money. Do you hear me? I want a divorce."

Still no response.

"And as for your secretary? She can go fuck herself as far as I'm concerned. The two of you deserve each other. I'm not footing the bill for anything anymore, especially if she's involved."

She stopped to listen, cupping her hand around her ear. She thought she heard a moan, but with all the noise from the outside, there was no real way of knowing.

"Gary, I hope your getting all this because I'm not saying it again. I'm done. *We're* done. And you're not getting one penny from me in the divorce. I don't care which one of your lawyer buddies you get – I'm gonna make sure you end up with nothing. Any judge'll see that I have grounds to leave your ass. Are you listening to me?"

There was movement in the pit. Gary was rousing.

"Kristy? Is that you? I love you, Kristy."

"You've got to be kidding me," Grace spat. "After all of this, *that's* where your mind is? Unbelievable."

"*Kris?*"

"You know…I should just leave you down there. When they come through that door, I should walk out of here and not even mention that you're in that hole."

She paused for a moment before adding her final thought on the matter.

"Some fuckin' honeymoon, huh, Gary?"

CHAPTER 33

The sun had risen completely by the time Gary's hallucinations of Kristy had subsided. It was almost 0900 and light was streaming in through the windows along the corridor. The brightness pierced the solemn atmosphere and edged its way along the body of the worm. The temperature had reached almost forty degrees, a practical heat wave compared to the previous hours of near freezing conditions. But trivial meteorological changes were not on Grace's radar.

She was preparing herself. And she was almost ready.

The entrance of the new day brought a stark reality to the gutted building. It was clear now just how empty and unwelcoming the station's interior was: no train cars, no clock tower, no kiosks or shops. It was a desperate husk of something that was once alive, but now stood as a placeholder, a tangible reminder of a horrific, devastating event that should have been laid to rest months ago.

Grace sat cross-legged at the edge of the hole. Her coat was zipped and buttoned and her woven hat had been pulled down around her face to cover her ears. Her mittens were tucked deep within her pockets and she held her purse tight against her stomach.

Gary's intermittent moans and calls for his office secretary had ceased. The delirium from the hemorrhage to his brain caused his blackouts to last for longer periods of time. Grace had estimated that the last one had clocked in at over twenty minutes. She had been keeping track. That was the last time he uttered Kristy's name and asked her to stay with him.

It didn't bother Grace anymore. If Gary wanted to dream about Kristy or anyone else at this point, she didn't care. She was beyond that now. She believed that she had transcended all of his garbage and all of his lies. While it was true that her low self-esteem and less-than courageous attitude was more than prevalent when she and Gary had first arrived, something *special* happened during the night. Something she might even dare to call *spiritual*. For whatever reason, these entities chose *her* and not Gary. As she contemplated this personal and emblematic ordination, she bowed her head in quasi-reverence.

The entire meaning of what happened to her when she was on the train still eluded her. She looked like someone had dumped a big bag of white flour over her head. The fact that this powdery residue was made up of the crushed bones and tissue of the dead never even entered her mind. There was nothing magical or supernatural about it. If she had known the origin of the substance, she would have gone mad.

Instead, she considered herself chosen. And with this *unholy gift* bestowed upon her, she surmised, what cause did she have to worry about Gary and his infidelity? She was destined for something far greater than to simply be Grace Wolf, wife of a Bloomington realtor from Illinois. Even though she had to endure a confusing childhood, an embarrassing and dreadful first marriage, and what would soon be a disastrous second one, Grace fully believed that she was fated for a future beyond her wildest dreams.

Something incredible had happened while she was in the train car. The fact that it has long been removed and burned was beside the point. *She* believed. It *did* exist for her. She was the exception to every rule.

"Gary."

No response.

"Gary, I want to tell you something before I leave."

She thought she heard a rustle of clothes or a muffled grunt from the depths of the hole. She held out her phone's light and could see the shape of his body.

"I'm just going to assume that you can hear what I'm saying. You don't have to answer. It's probably better if you don't because it's not going to make a difference anyway. I wanted to tell you that I've decided to leave. I'm not waiting for the police or firefighters or anybody else. I've been blessed, Gary. I realize that now and I've accepted it. Whoever died in here has given me some kind of special power. I know that might sound crazy to you, but I can feel it and I believe it to be true. I also know that they're going to let me walk out those doors."

She paused, hoping to hear some sort of reaction, but was met with silence. She continued.

"They must have seen something in me because they chose *me* over you. If it were any other time or place, you would have been chosen. But not *here*; not *this* time. Why else would you be down there all broken and mangled while I'm up here with hardly a scratch on me?"

An eerie groan rose up from the hole. She stopped to listen.

"Gary?"

Again, silence.

"Anyway, after I leave, I'll let someone know that you're down there. Okay? I want you to know that I'll send help. I mean, just because I'm done with you doesn't mean I'm *completely* heartless," she smirked.

She stood and gazed into the recess where her husband lay unconscious on the ground.

"Someone should rescue you within an hour or so. We can work out the details of the divorce after we're both back home. Goodbye, Gary."

Grace adjusted her coat and hat once more and walked purposefully down the long worm-like corridor toward the mouth of the building. The two large doors that were locked from either side now stood before her. With a deep breath and a new conviction that had eluded her only hours ago, Grace grabbed both handles of the doors and pulled them toward her.

Astonishingly, they opened. Blinding rays of sun and a burst of fresh December air immediately washed over her. She squinted and stepped over the station's threshold, out into the world again. A smile spread across her lips as she closed her eyes and raised her face toward the sky. A half-second later, a man began screaming at the engineering supervisor. Unfortunately, the man couldn't hear him over the detonation devices that had just been engaged.

Apparently, Pieter Hinter thought he had seen the figure of a woman appear in front of the doors just before the building imploded.

Epilogue

4 December - Article from the Rain Germany Gazette:

In accordance with all municipalities involved, the Rain Bahnhof has been razed as of 2 December. Cooperation among many facilities allowed the demolition and the following clean-up to proceed without incident. Neither anything of value nor any personal items had been found in the aftermath.

A committee will be formed over the next few weeks in order to help determine potential concepts for the future of the site. If you are interested in assisting, please plan to attend. Any questions may be directed to Mr. Heinz Muller, Interim.

A separate memorial service will be held for the family of Sergeant Pieter Hinter, who was found dead from a self-inflicted gunshot wound on the evening of 2 December. A police investigation is underway.

About the Author

Sue Rovens spends her days working among 1.6 million books in Milner Library at Illinois State University. Her evenings and weekends are taken up by a multitude of other activities, some of which involve writing, running, and watching movies. If animals are involved in any way, it's all the better.

Track 9 is her second novel.

If you enjoyed this book, please consider posting a review on Amazon, Goodreads, or any other social media outlet.

If you want more information on Sue Rovens, her other books, or her latest work, please visit inacornerdarkly.blogspot.com or email her at srovens@yahoo.com.

Thank you!

22298431R00133

Made in the USA
Columbia, SC
30 July 2018